SCUTTLEBUTT

Confessions of a Navy
Air Traffic Controller

BILL HENRY

Copyright © 2023 Bill Henry
All rights reserved
First Edition

PAGE PUBLISHING
Conneaut Lake, PA

First originally published by Page Publishing 2023

ISBN 979-8-89157-039-9 (pbk)
ISBN 979-8-89157-066-5 (digital)

Printed in the United States of America

Preface

Events in our lives occur daily. Time marches on. Somewhere within our mind, as if on a seesaw, these events—some remembered, others long forgotten—rise to the surface as memories. Recognizing the context they add to our personal history, we choose to hang onto these memories. The more context, the more well-rounded your history becomes.

Resurrected and recalled, your memories in the here and now provide details with your current hindsight to support them. These memories can be refreshed and translated for use.

A book of fiction, the reconstruction of events in this book was based on the life and times of the author. Names and certain situations have been slightly altered, contingent on presenting a coherent viewpoint of military and civilian air traffic control during the timespan encompassed.

Spring 1976

The 8,000 ft. runway was positioned directly in front of the tower window with a panoramic view of surrounding mountains in the background. Blue waters of the bay washed against three sides of the airport. The local flight pattern, where pilots needing practice with repetitive touch-and -go, was busy with each aircraft climbing to 1,200 ft. on the downwind leg. The five aircraft currently in the pattern consisted of two A-7s (attack-oriented, single-engine jet), one F-8 (fighter-oriented, single-engine jet), one P-3 (patrol-oriented, four-engine turboprop), and an E-2 (dual-engine electronic reconnaissance aircraft that has the saucer-shaped, revolving antenna positioned on top.)

Plugging in my headset, I got the brief and began my shift. Within ten minutes, the E-2 made a full stop, followed soon thereafter by one of the A-7s. Jets, much faster than the P-3, were flying a tighter pattern within the four-engine prop's wider and slower evolution—all working smoothly.

Dusk in full swing, the setting sun dipped into the East China Sea west of Subic Bay, Philippines. Brilliant pink rays of a fading sun reflected striations reminiscent of a Japanese symbol from an era in the not-too-distant past. This very bay was a Japanese navy stronghold once General McArthur was defeated prior to the Bataan Death March which began in this very area.

To simulate an aircraft carrier's capability at sea, our 8,000 ft. runway was equipped with two arresting gear cables, across the runway, approximately 1,200 ft. from either end of the runway. All naval aircraft used on carriers are equipped with a tailhook, which the pilot lowers when landing on the carrier or in an emergency—equipped runways. When an arrested landing is utilized, airport personnel are required to assist the aircraft and reset the cable, rendering the runway closed temporarily.

Runway lighting was activated, adding to an already picturesque tropical island sunset. The F-8 lifted from the runway's departure end utilizing its afterburner capability, shooting a 20 ft. burst of flames out it's aft end. Turning a shortened base-leg to final, the A-7's pilot advised his aircraft had a hydraulic warning indication and would need to make an arrested landing in the E-28 arresting gear at the approach end of the runway. Clearance issued; the tower activated the emergency response procedures after which I sent the P-3 up to 2,500 ft. then climbed the F-8 to a 2,000 ft. delta pattern for holding due to impending runway closure. The A-7's tailhook engaged the cable, prompting a mad dash by flight support personnel toward the scene to commence disengagement from the cable. Runway closed, I cleared two vehicles to cross the runway at midfield toward the scene of the emergency. One of the vehicles stopped on the runway at midfield, the driver stating his engine stalled. The other pickup arrived at the A-7 engagement.

Overhead, the F-8 circled once in its holding pattern, entering downwind with the transmission, "Cubi Point Tower, Red Fox 69 has experienced a flameout commencing descent for the runway." Holy crap! This guy is straddling a guided rocket whose one engine just died, descending through 1,200 ft. with no room or altitude to attempt a restart. His options are to somehow guide what is now a "lead-sled" toward the runway or punch out by activating the ejection system. If the pilot chose ejection, the impending wreckage with the F-8's position would take out a third of Olongapo, undoubtedly wiping out hundreds of innocent Filipino civilians in their homes—not good. Once again, the tower activated the emergency procedures for the second time within three minutes for a different aircraft.

I told the pilot of the F-8 the last thing he wanted to hear, "Runway is closed."

The tone of his reply indicated the dire situation he knew he was in. "Thirty seconds...tops" was the chilled response. No rookie here—this pilot's squadron, in support of US personnel, had flown harrowing missions against communist MiG-21s over the Mekong Delta. He knew his desperate situation down to the seconds.

SCUTTLEBUTT

I switched my communication console to the FM frequency the flight support personnel were monitoring with the transmission, "Push the A-7 away from the runway centerline toward the edge and remain clear. F-8 possibly landing in twenty-five seconds." Acknowledged, the A-7 began a slow, creeping pace toward the runway's edge. I next demanded the stalled pickup, still on the runway at midfield, "Push the vehicle toward the edge of the runway *immediately!*" It was at least a 100 ft. task. Back to the frequency the F-8 was monitoring, I advised the pilot that the runway was still "foul" (closed), yet I included the A-7's position in addition to the location of the arresting gear at the departure end of the runway.

The F-8 pilot, as well as I, knew he had one chance to "thread the needle." Trimming the ailerons with the slightest touch; gliding this now-powerless, descending "rocket" over the A-7's position; high enough that a touchdown approaching midfield—a much faster approach than normal—would make it mandatory to engage the roll-out arresting cable. If the F-8's hook skipped that cable (quite common), his aircraft's speed would propel the F-8 off the runway's end into the awaiting sea. As per NATOPS and FAA 7110.8, this maneuver wasn't legal nor suggested in any way for tape-recording purposes.

In this high-stakes game, his quick judgment of the aircraft's dead-weight, glideslope potential versus the sharp angle overflying an A-7 approximately 1,300 ft. beyond the approach end had to be spot on. Yes, if successful, it would save the navy an F-8 but without propulsion, heavy aircraft succumb to gravity like anything else. Life expectancy of any pilot surviving an ejection had improved; a substantial percentage didn't make it. Civilian casualties had to be the overwhelming factor, flashing like a billboard in New York Times Square, all behind this pilot's eyes. The lethal hand he'd suddenly been dealt had maybe three seconds for his decision.

With a closed runway, my hands were tied; I could not issue a landing clearance. The status of the runway was issued in case he decided to throw the book out the window. From the pilot's perspective, very valuable real estate still existed there. Question was, could his skill get him and the F-8 to it? He'd made his choice.

Descending into a steep dogleg to final, the F-8's committed flight path overflew the A-7, by now hugging the runway edge. More than the highest-ever rollercoaster plunging from its steepest angle, this pilot rode his "potentially expensive coffin" essentially on wings and a prayer, passing the pickup still 10 ft. from the runway's edge.

Observing this marvel of machine, man, and fate, I keyed the transmitter issuing a wind check. The departure-end, arresting gear successfully engaged with a solid hook exactly thirty seconds from when he stated he would. Through the cockpit's canopy, the pilot observed only the last set of runway-edge lighting, before his invitation into a now dark abyss of sea was boldly declined…for now. One chance, life on the line—he'd penetrated the needle's eye. In this business, timing is everything! Vietnam-era, US Navy pilots were masters of the sky.

Getting here…

This is dedicated to those that go down to the sea in ships.

Fall 1972

Emmerson, Lake, & Palmer's "From the Beginning" (1972) played melodically through the car's radio. "It's all clear, you were meant to be here, from the beginning…" The lyrics were heard by four people within the car. Unusual silence by all, listening to the prophetic meaning that was not lost on any of us. Yet recent turnabout measures by the US government had warned of peril ahead. New draft eligibility measures from the government had begun putting our hopes and dreams on ice.

Campus had been left miles behind as we sought peace of mind. The '64 Pontiac Catalina sat completely obscured by darkness at the end of a dirt road, which led into an immense soybean field. Four occupants were inside, grateful for enough solitude to reflect on impending decisions young adult men all over the country were forced to consider as of late—their future.

Four years older than the others, Chris spoke from the backseat, "Focus on those stars a minute…they seem to multiply the longer you stare at them. It was the same way in Nam. The makeshift rack I returned to after every mission had a window I'd stare out at night… believing I'd never make it back here." Chris had been a helicopter crewman serving his one year in country between '69 and '70 after the Tet Offensive move by the North Vietnamese.

Gerald, next to the other open window in the backseat, remarked, "Didn't we come out here to forget about Nam for a few hours?"

"You're right…wish I could turn it off…24-7," Chris admitted.

I removed a joint from the enclosed tin container which had "Wacky Tobacky" emblazoned on the top. "Maybe this will soothe the woes temporarily," I said, handing it to him.

Eric tuned in KNOE on the Pontiac's radio. "Does your car's battery have enough juice for a few more minutes?"

"I just replaced it a couple weeks ago in the dorm parking lot, we're good," I answered as "Let It Be" by the Beatles (1970) appropriately settled the air.

Orlo and BJ walked into the dorm room as if it was their own. Formalities had been left behind last year after we'd met as freshmen at Northeast Louisiana University (NLU) in Monroe. "Is the birthday party still on for tonight?" Orlo asked.

"Lane scored a lid this morning, so if you bring a case of Budweiser, I'll go in half. We should be set." Nineteen for two months, I was in my second year at college. Navigating some tough courses the last few semesters, I'd somehow made the dean's list—similar, I guess, to honor rolls back home. In other words, so what?

Eric, my roommate, flipped the album "Benefit" by Jethro Tull (1970) over on the turntable saying, "BJ, bring back some ice for the beer this time. My future is on the line tonight. Drinking warm beer could be a bad omen." The college deferment, some of us had utilized since turning eighteen to avoid booby-trapped trails through the jungles of Vietnam, had vanished. Promises from Richard Nixon to wound-down the war seemed to be another one of his growing lists of lies, earning him the nickname Tricky Dicky.

Later that evening, our group huddled around a television in the dorm room during Orlo's version of a birthday party. Despite the Bud empties filling the shitcan and a couple joints revolving around the room, rogue waves of anxiety engulfed each of us. We watched the cage spin. This highly publicized event, mandated by the hounds of war, was to determine, out of 365 days, the order the birthday draft notices would be sent out. The question on everyone's mind: would anyone among us be walking the plank?

Eric said, "Nixon's serving us up on a platter for his own benefit, I tell ya. The guy's a crook...look at his nose...can always tell one by their nose. This warm beer tastes like horse piss. Where's BJ? Can't trust him to get ice."

I knew Eric's appraisal of our president was spot on. Nixon seemed two-faced—saying publicly what his supporters wanted to hear but conducting his own agenda under the shadows of night. Supporters of the war harped on the domino theory; communism was chipping away at small nations—a malignancy which must be stopped. Young American men were now pawns being utilized in a small country's dispute between its northern and southern regions. Men around the country, eighteen years and up, watched as their future tumbled one by one, out of the spinning wire cage. The twenty-first draw was September 26...SOB! The cancer which had plagued our country for eight long years, drawing young men into its deadly clutches would soon be my impending diagnosis.

Within a month, my campus PO box had a letter from the US government addressed to Jess Harper. I was to report to Little Rock for my physical. The bus ride there languished, my mind on a seesaw between rising to the occasion like John Wayne storming some Hollywood beach versus an elimination by physical handicap, which I didn't have. Much too exuberant to tell me I passed, examiners sent me back to Monroe, Louisiana. "Masters of War" by Bob Dylan (1963) was playing in my head the whole trip.

The campus remained vibrant as ever. Of the guys attending last month's dorm birthday party, I had come up with the shortest straw. I felt shrouded in fog trudging from class to class like a zombie from *Night of the Living Dead* (1968), which we watched again last month in the dorm room.

Uncle Sam's irrefutable invitation, tipping the scales, outweighed the hard-won balanced position here at college. No wonder I felt a slow-to-medium boil building daily. With an afternoon free of classes, I escaped the campus seeking peace of mind. Half a joint later, with the Door's "Riders on the Storm" (1967), playing on the radio, my eyes landed on a sign unnoticed before, one offering a slight alternative. As my foot applied the brake, my mind began to race. On top of being robbed of a college education, the mere act of Nixon's coercion demanding compliance yanked my chain. By walking through this door, Nixon still had me but I, possibly, could have some say-so concerning the outcome.

Sitting in the US Navy's recruiting office, posters depicted exotic locales. As in the crackerjack uniform with white dixie-cup hat emblazoned on the wall, the recruiter delivered his sales pitch. Gambling to beat the inevitable draft notice heading toward my mailbox, I still found myself edging toward the exit until the president's picture on the wall—his long, Pinocchio-nose seemingly out of joint, stopped me. Reality slapped my face, demanding I take this option—I did. Next four years were signed over to the USN. "Follow me," said the navy recruiter. My first order: following the recruiter through the hall into an exam room. It occurred to me I'll be having a lot of those barked my way. They sat me down, still high as a kite, for a performance exam. For Christ's sake! I shouldn't do this now, but I couldn't tell this guy that.

"I have an important college exam in twenty minutes. I need to do this tomorrow," I lied.

The sailor looked at me in a cock-eyed way. "Jess, the job you will do in the navy depends on the results ascertained from this exam. As of five minutes ago, you're operating on navy time. Pick up the pencil. You have two hours," he said, closing the door. After the exam, he gave me a brochure. "Choose overnight," he said, "you're eligible for any job except nuclear submarines." They needn't have worried about that.

Not having flown in an aircraft yet, I'd never pondered how they were controlled, but there it was, listed in the brochure. On a lark, air traffic control it was. After years of "little" then "pony" league baseball, I'd soon come to learn, I'd just stepped up to the proverbial plate and finally hit a homerun.

Guys at the dorm thought I'd be heading to Canada. They threw a going-away shindig anyway—the age when a party for any excuse was natural.

Naval Training Command, Boot Camp Company 043, Orlando, Florida—January 1973

After eight long years of death on both sides, the US couldn't stop a never-ending flow of enemy troops and equipment using the Ho Chi Minh trail. US troop levels fluctuated while peace talks repeatedly floundered. North Vietnam, with China and the USSR's aid, had the US between a rock and a hard place. Nixon knew it, as well as people eligible for the draft. In Nixon's mind, peace protesters at home were as much an enemy as North Vietnamese regulars.

Back in '69, anti-war protestors had formed the Moratorium, an organized group more palatable on Joe Public. Until then, television coverage had mostly shown long-hairs smoking a joint while burning draft cards. Obviously, it took someone appearing clean-cut getting bashed in the head by Nixon's thugs to mount sympathy to their cause. It had worked. Nixon had planned to escalate the war, but the successful protests had swayed public opinion against any such gamble. In fact, they were the nails in the coffin for Nixon's war effort. He managed to drag out troop withdrawals for three more years, all the while keeping draft boards operating. Eventually Nixon's rampage ended. The US commander in chief's impending doom in the Watergate investigation didn't herald inspiration to lay one's body down for the US' cause either.

Life in the US Navy for this sailor began in Orlando's boot camp. Written on the quarterdeck's wall was the goal of the sailor: "Control the rudder so the proper course and ship's heading is maintained." Words of warning—when at sea your actions can mean life or death. With dropping a fishing line over the side my only experience in a boat, I had a lot to learn.

Free will, independence, was targeted for diminishment during boot camp. Cohesiveness of the "unit mentality" should replace it. Just how that mindset surgery would take place were my concern. The first morning, some assholes pitched empty metal shitcans down the aisle of our barracks at 4:00 a.m. Their shock and awe first wave. After a whole ten minutes to eat breakfast, we headed toward an industrial method of hair removal: buzz cutting. Shoulder, waist, just below the ear, all lengths of hair in 1973 whether bushy, wavy, kinky, or straight lay six inches deep on the floor around at least a dozen barbers with electric clippers at full-bore.

These boot camp guidelines requiring everyone react to procedures in a required manner when needed—lives depended on it—were essential, as per the force-fed reel after reel of *Victory at Sea* (1952) episodes from WWII. With concurrence, I understood their point, yet my own independent mind would never be relinquished. Nineteen years navigating Louisiana Bible Belt's stubborn bigots, refusing equal and civil rights to people of color, proved my point. Mercy on those victimized; their daily experience had to be tormenting. It was horrendous to some of us, helplessly watching it happen. Simply existing within such a dominating mindset, while not succumbing to its permeating, racists ideals, reminded me now, choosing which Kool-Aid to drink, was possible. Uncle Sam's uninvited intrusion into my college environment was, after all, what got me here.

Close order drill; small arms training; sound powered telephone operation; lifesaving techniques at sea; gas masks; physical training; firefighting; knot tying; field-day inspections and proper uniforms were only a portion of the eight weeks preparation to enter the US Navy. Divided into companies, the hundreds of new recruits conformed to each company commander, as if he were Moses coming down off the mountain. Ours was BM1 Hudsucker, a boatswain mate with a chest full of medals from various combat operations in South Vietnam. Like an old high-school coach, Hudsucker was firm but fair. He had filled in as a Gunner's Mate on a patrol boat, flushing out "gooks" as he called them, on the Mekong River Delta about fifty miles inland from its mouth in the South China Sea.

Through weeks of competition—every facet of training graded—our company was in a tie for first place or flag company. Fifteen-minute smoke breaks were given, prompting those who didn't to join the smoking fiends. "Smoke on the Water" by Deep Purple (1972) played in the recreation room. From the second eyes opened each a.m. until they closed in the p.m., each sailor was graded on his actions. Some recruits excelled, be it meeting physical standards, marching and drill practice, or correct answers in seamanship terminology. Others cruised at their dependably mediocre speed of just getting by, and a few simply couldn't cut it. Those at this frayed end of the rope were, let's say given a "pep-talk" by each company commander. Non-complying slackers were then kicked out of their existing company and promptly added to the next company. The new bunkmate in the rack overhead was such—withdrawn when approached, obviously disturbed, only participating with reluctance.

The Swedish meatball concoction served over the rice on my tray reminded me of the stint, two weeks prior, when I was detailed to the chow hall for service week. Navy's recipe for the Swedish dish, on Tuesday of that week, involved cutting and chopping parts, when combined I knew would never cross my lips. Today, starved as I was feeling, I couldn't force myself to pick up the fork. My new top bunkmate, his name Travers spelled out in the stencil above his shirt pocket, was finishing his portion from his tray. From across the table, I offered him my uneaten Swedish meatballs. Accepting my tray, one corner of his lips tipped upward as he mumbled, "'Preciate it." First words I'd heard him mutter.

"Some things I just can't squeeze down the pipes," I said, expecting no reply.

"My mother's favorite dish back in Indianapolis," Travers said just above his breath.

"Hey, look, if there's anything I…"

Hudsucker called out, "That's ten…Co. 043, report to the parade field in three minutes."

"I'm in the rack below yours, don't hesitate if you need something." I let him know before joining the exodus for the door. I left the table. Travers was unmoved, savoring each bite as if it was his last. Co. 043 lined up, commencing close-order drill absent Travers and Hudsucker.

The last thing prior to hitting the rack each night, all sailors scrubbed their white hats before hanging them out to dry on the third-floor roof of our barracks. Reaching for clothespins to attach my hat, I noticed Travers on my immediate left make a quick movement pushing me aside, as he dashed toward the roof's edge about fifteen feet away. As Travers flew past, I had no time to react before he sailed, arms extended out, into a headfirst nosedive, out of sight. Three seconds of a curdling death scream sealed off with blunt-force impact. Stunned! We looked at each other—speechless. Who or whatever drove this man over the edge, his life had become cheap enough to self-extinguish it. Security interviewed all of us on the roof. I tried sleeping but couldn't stay in my rack that night.

Hudsucker called the company into a huddle, saying Travers had been dealing with overwhelming issues which had gotten too much for him to handle. If any of us needed someone to talk to, Hudsucker was available. His "get over it" attitude seemed cheap; I just wasn't buying it. "BM1 Hudsucker, sir (he wasn't an officer, but in boot camp, company commanders demanded it), yesterday Travers finally opened up to me in the chow hall, now he's a stain on the concrete outside our barracks. May we know what you talked with him about enroute to the parade field?" Taken aback, his eyes shifted as if guilt controlled them.

"I never talked to Travers after chow," he lied. "Like I said, I'm available if you need counseling."

I wanted to get the hell out of that place, fast.

After learning the knack of trading "self" for "group" achievement, introduction to seafaring, and dealing with death, Co. 043 was awarded flag company. What else but toilet paper could provide such satisfaction?

Naval Aviation Training Command, Naval Air Station Glynco, Georgia—March 1973

Pine forests stretch, virtually nonstop, throughout the southeast corner of Georgia, finally reaching the Atlantic coast. Accessible islands, such as St. Simons, are nearby. Outside Brunswick was Glynco Naval Air Station, where I was detailed for air traffic control technical training. Time to rectify my cobwebs of ignorance.

According to Steely Dan's new song playing on the Pontiac Catalina's radio, I should be "Reeling in the Years" (1973). The road trip to Glynco from Louisiana reminded me I was just getting started. Open-bay barracks from the early '60s still beat the rigors of boot camp. Technical information concerning aircraft systems; communication capabilities; navigational aids; ground-radar capabilities; and rules of aircraft separation in flight, as well as, on landing and takeoff, appeared written in Mandarin Chinese—I had twelve weeks. Navy detailers at the Pentagon decided who went where if we made it through at all. Detailers could be kind with a prestigious billet to an ideal air station where the best positions for advancements existed—dependent, of course, upon information absorption and reaction therewith. On the other hand, any lackluster performance—24-7 field days on an oil can out of Shanghai.

Despite pressure, life was good. At least the tonsils of BM1 Hudsucker weren't slapping my face. New music releases from Led Zeppelin's "Houses of the Holy" (1973) and David Bowie's "The Rise and Fall of Ziggy Stardust and the Spiders from Mars" (1973) kept us mesmerized. As at college back in Monroe, any free time to get away from the base, I took. Of course, the Catalina provided access to others I invited; friends were made, and Tim McCracken was one. St. Simon's Island offered beaches nearby or events in Jacksonville, Florida were a couple hours away.

Mc held the exit doors from the theatre open after we'd finished *The Poseidon Adventure* (1972). Walking through the Georgia rain to the car, he asked, "Battleships in Pearl Harbor remained upside down with people inside, right?"

"Yes, your point being?"

"I'm just saying the navy proved *The Poseidon Adventure* was feasible."

"Possible not probable. McCracken, you're so gung ho. Probably a narc…you know, you must tell me if I ask you to your face, don't you?"

"Jess, my favorite uncle's a FAA controller in upstate New York. I've put five different aircraft carrier models together since age twelve."

"Five carrier models? Three letters, OCD."

"Just combining two things I respect…putting two pieces of some puzzle together, I guess."

"Most guys in bootcamp said shore duty is better than sea duty."

"Jess, how are you going to see the world on shore duty?"

Untested limits, those irksome hurdles everyone encounters along the path of life, where a good balance between hard work and hard play is required. That balance will be tested at some point—some people more than others. Movies from yesteryears had reenforced the levels of drunken debauchery military members could reach on liberty, especially sailors. If off-kilter, where play was allowed to blend with work, perceptive navy instructors weeded out those unable to "trim the sail," so to speak. Two years back in Monroe had been sufficient to hone the skill of moderation. Granted, parents at home would have blown a twenty-amp fuse if any hint of such deviltry was occurring on their dime. Understandable—life's little eccentricities, waywardness, or nonconformities, however classified, was going to begin for me at some point. Reefer, although illegal, became a go-to accelerant toward hard play for its advantages over alcohol. Yes, consequences were dire; somehow that only added a thrill to smoking it. Such situations provided reality-based character studies. Since the first semesters of college, it had become apparent how people confronted responsibility revealed their dependability. Each morning became a reckoning who could handle themselves in the job the navy was there to teach.

Three weeks before graduation, McCracken claimed his old VW bug could make it the two hours down to Jacksonville Beach the next weekend. "Harper, what's more important—getting somewhere or the way you get there?"

"Depends…you and your questions, just say where you're going with this."

"I've had my VW bug over at the auto hobby shop since arriving, getting it back in shape for after graduation. Let's test it out this weekend on a trip to Jax Beach." He was right; Friday night we stayed on the beach hitting the murky surf early as the sun was rising. That morning, I felt like you can imagine—virtually sleepless overnight on a blanket under cloudy skies. Any crud accumulated was quickly washed away after an initial splash in the murky waves lapping Jax Beach.

"Can your caffeine addiction be tested for a few hours?" Mc asked returning to the blanket.

"Noon's good for me."

"Last night's pizza's still packing the load for me. Noon it is. Jess, I asked Master Chief 'Ski what my chances of getting orders to a nuclear aircraft carrier were."

"You and I have done well throughout the course. Those so-called 'dream sheets' mentioned, where we put down locations we'd prefer, may benefit us if we've given one hundred percent."

"Yeah, 'Ski said conventional carriers were a dying breed but still had to be utilized as long as possible."

"I'm sure we're going to have more time at sea than either one of us could ever want…now let's go get wet in it."

"Nuclear is the future…we'll be there before you know it," Mc said turning toward the surf.

The craving for coffee battled its way back into my frontal lobe as the sore back, created from last night's bed of soggy sand, reminded me I should relax a few here on the blanket.

Repeatedly falling asleep on the blanket, waking up, and hitting the waves, I looked for Mc and never locating him. Probably met some girl undoubtedly talking about his romance with aircraft carriers. Noon came and went, and the need for caffeine having manifested into a ten-penny nail being driven in my forehead. Mc was surely involved in a conversation somewhere. Even with assistance from others up and down the beach, looking and calling his name—no response. Hours later, my hopes dashed; Mc's body washed ashore. I identified Tim McCracken's body, found about two-hundred yards down from our blanket. If only I'd been there to help. Later, it was determined that Mc had an epileptic seizure in the waves that morning. Mc hadn't reported this condition, as per his family, when contacted. It would have been an eliminating factor for his goal of air traffic controller. I drove his old VW the two hours north, back to Glynco, knowing Mc would have been proud it made it. Mc's nuclear aircraft carrier sailed from Jax Beach that Saturday, returning only once more to a deserted island around the world.

Graduation was around the corner. People I'd become friends with struggling alongside lengthy study sessions would be going separate ways. This depressing realization would sadly reoccur repeatedly over the next twenty years—people briefly intersecting, sharing moments etched into memories, then gone. Two weeks later, I landed orders to Master Jet Base Lemoore. "Going To California" by Led Zeppelin (1971).

Driving back to Louisiana, I stopped at Jax Beach, "letting my freak-flag fly, felt like I owed it to someone," (Crosby, Stills, Nash, & Young 1970). In my mind, I owed Mc. Revisiting the scene made hairs on my neck come to attention. Grimy surf washed my bare feet—the oddity of calling upon a dead person's spirit, totally a new experience. "I'm betting on you somehow hearing me, Tim…sorry I wasn't there when you needed me. Your family came for your VW. Got orders to California. You'll never be forgotten." Got in the '64 Pontiac and headed west on I-10.

Naval Air Station Lemoore, California—June 1973

The US Navy had hundreds of ships at sea protecting sea-lanes and launching air raids against the North Vietnamese. As the US Air Force, the USN also has military airports along various seacoasts which are the home base for carrier aircraft and support personnel. Differences are huge between sea duty—working on a ship—versus shore duty at a military base. Sea duty—where the sail meets the wind, sailors and their ship must be mobile to perform their function. Shore duty is more akin to a stationary civilian job. In fairness to all, sailors realize every two or three years, they will rotate between sea and shore duty.

Surrounded by farming activity in the San Joaquin Valley, Lemoore Naval Base is colossal—at least a three-mile bus trip one-way from the barracks to the airport. Ranked as a master jet base, not only for its number of daily operations but the complexity involved, Lemoore was where the action was. Every type of surveillance and detection, bombing and attack, but mostly fighter jets, were actively on radar approach or within the local tower pattern as I arrived. It was a gah-lee, jaw-dropping gomer moment, seeing the actual aircraft from manuals at ATC school here at my proving ground. The effort put in to get here could pay off.

As with any job, the new employee must prove to management their reliability and ability to learn the job. I quickly determined there was a line of controllers, in which I now stood last, to begin training in the control tower. My enthusiasm to sail over the hurdle of qualification had to wait for nine months; a long time to watch others ahead make their attempt, some successful, others not.

Months as office secretary then base operations dispatcher provided time to learn basic information, make friends, and work alongside civilian employees who eagerly trained me as the rookie. Regina was one such civilian in base ops who became a friend. She was dating a pilot in one of the A-7 squadrons; in other words, senseless for my mind to even entertain the natural thought. Yet, there it dwelled, wasting precious space.

Yosemite was two hours east up in the Sierra Nevada mountains; the Pacific coastline was two hours west if you weren't walking, as in my case. My only avenue off base was a duty van, which made the trip up Highway 41 thirty-eight miles to Fresno bus station and civilian airport, supporting incoming and outgoing sailors. Here I was surrounded by the Golden State of California. I'd busted my ass in ATC school to earn, but no private transportation to enjoy it with. Hence, I studied ATC regulations, jogged along obscure trails with jackrabbits, and saved money.

Chief of Naval Operations, Admiral Zumwalt, got along good with sailors serving on land and at sea during his time at the helm, mostly because he communicated his intentions. His method was the Z-Gram, sent out to all whenever he had something to say. Of the other branches in the military, Zumwalt held out the longest from reinstituting rigid, grooming standards when personnel returned from the war zone. Sailors noticed the difference. Z-Grams from the CNO allowed full beards, even handlebar mustaches if the genes of any sailor naturally allowed such.

Spring of '74. Stretch, all six-foot-five of a lanky sailor, whom Billy Gibbons of ZZ Top could model his facial hair after, had the picture-perfect handlebar mustache. He also had a Honda 500 cc motorcycle for sale. Greenbacks for wheels and spokes, I saddled the wind—the Golden State awaited. With a steep learning curve, the cycle and I became a well-oiled machine touring up and down the coastline or cycling up to Fresno's theatres for new screen flicks—*Jaws* (1975) and *The Exorcist* (1973)—two movies having the most profound effect on my psyche ever.

Nixon learned he wasn't above the law; California's Zodiac Killer, as well as the Golden State Killer, left unaccounted for deaths in their wake while still practicing their grisly hobby; Robin Trower and Peter Frampton were great guitarists playing on K-FIG Fresno radio; Patty Hearst, recently kidnapped by the SLA, brandished a Thompson submachine gun while robbing a bank with her unlikely new cohorts; I began training in the control tower. All radio frequencies recorded, each radio transmission made had to conform to FAA or USN phraseology and rule application. Ear cruncher headsets were still utilized. Within my duty section, I was assigned to a qualified controller whose mission was my qualification. Yes, personal effort and study came into play, but AC2 Stokes' relentless training method was highly beneficial.

With combat-airstrike aircraft returning from Vietnam, the intensity was humbling. These pilots had met life-and-death situations every time they flew their mission over Southeast Asia. It was in their self-interest to become one with their aircraft or end up in a rice-paddy crater. Russian Migs made comparable dogfight opponents, but the deadliest foe was the surface-to-air missiles China brought to the air battle.

Back stateside now, these US Navy pilots still had to maintain currency. Top-notch aviators, any of these pilots could have qualified for the Blue Angles on any given day. Controllers must take into consideration the various speeds each of these different type aircraft must maintain to accomplish their training. This consideration becomes critical in your pattern strategy.

"The airport traffic area belongs to you. If you need to break off an inbound radar approach, tell the radar controller and do it. Shut down visual approaches, tell approach control. Stop departures... you can. Better have a damned good reason. Point is, you control it," Stokes explained. "Run your VFR (visual flight rules) pattern here at the airport, sequencing them into the straight-in IFR (instrument flight rules) traffic. The IFR traffic must maintain at least three miles separation. You must separate your tower pattern from each other, and the IFR traffic with the established runway separation in the 7110.8 FAA handbook," Stokes instructed. The complexity was intriguing. I had to keep pursuing this.

Qualified on two of the three tower positions, I was then training on local control where all things flying within five miles under 3,000 ft. were in my jurisdiction. The last jet of this event held short of runway 32L for departure into the FCLP pattern (field carrier landing practice). This runway was equipped with a Fresnel lens, a shipboard optical landing system assisting the pilot's line up for a precise positioning as the aircraft descends to touchdown. All this effort of simulation on land-based airports detailing shipboard operations was to prepare navy pilots precisely for the hazardous act of landing a jet aboard a flight deck rising and falling with each wave at sea. This lens sat adjacent the runway next to a full-sized, painted outline of an aircraft carrier on Lemoore's runway. This outline had flush lighting within the runway surface, for night usage—as this night.

To my chagrin, Regina married her pilot yet continued working in base operations while her husband was in training here at the base, flying the navy's attack jet, the A-7 Corsair. Earlier that evening, I'd stopped by base operations to say hello to Regina. She looked radiant, marriage obviously agreeing with her.

Weather that night was clear. After two hours of training, one more jet held short of the runway for departure before I was to be relieved. Creating a space in the pattern, I cleared the jet holding short for departure with his acknowledgment, unplugged my headset, and moved over to ground control. While doing so, the jet I had cleared departed and turned downwind into the local tower pattern. The new local controller called the jet, now beyond base leg. No response—repeated attempts failed. The controller activated the emergency overriding guard channel. No response. The A-7 attack jet began descending; despite emergency transmissions to pull up, all controllers in the tower turned to observe. A fireball illuminated the night sky from ground level. Baptism by fire! His last—my fourth to witness in three years.

No meaning can be found in tragedy, only our response to it. Training helped with the mouth-agape, slack-jaw stance, hoping the pilot ejected. At ground control, I leaned over and grabbed the crash phone—a phone I was familiar with, not from situations like this but the daily test we conducted, ensuring it connected to all stations needed to respond in an emergency. Stations on the crash net—fire department, medical, base operations, and others—picked up their crash phone to hear my declaration: *crash, crash, crash*, aircraft call sign, and position. Acknowledgments followed. Base operations was silent—no response. Aware of her husband's call sign, Regina had picked up the crash phone in base operations only to collapse after hearing my announcement. Intuitively, she knew her husband was dead.

Investigations concluded the pilot developed vertigo before reaching base leg. It was theorized he'd lost his line of horizon, became so confused he didn't respond to radio calls, and flew his jet into the ground. Like gravity, death respects no barriers. Regina didn't return to her job after that night. No opportunity to give condolences, nor confess it was I to whom her husband uttered his last words.

The movie *Dirty Harry* (1971) along with the television drama *Streets of San Francisco* (1972) primed interest in visiting the city. The bay, nestled within the hills, is as beautiful as the city it serves. The Golden Gate Bridge, like a ribbon holding together the two sides of the bay's entrance, completes the package. My mind's eye observed the long-ago schooners delivering explorers, then traders over the centuries—voices of generations whispering in the constant breeze. Via bus from Fresno, I spent the day walking those streets of San Francisco; evading bus station predators; jumping onto streetcars; and refusing con artists on Market Street pawning their stolen watches. Later that night, headed back to Fresno in the "backseat of a Greyhound bus going down Highway 41," Allman Brothers (1973), I realized San Francisco, despite the seedier side, was absolute eye candy for anyone with an eye for beautiful scenery. I returned multiple times and once to the Cow Palace Arena for an Eric Clapton concert. Eric had come so close to dying from heroin addiction. Everyone with an ear for guitar knew he had much more to contribute to the world from the recent LP *461 Ocean Boulevard* (1974), containing the hit "I Shot the Sheriff." San Francisco's rolling hills and sailboats on the bay continued luring me toward repeated visits.

Dad and Mom drove over from Louisiana to visit. I reserved a room in the Navy Lodge where they stayed for about a week in between our trips over to Monterey then north up Highway 1 into San Francisco. Dad got to see one last time the bottom of the Golden Gate Bridge; an angle he'd seen the first time on a troop ship leaving SF during WWII, all the while, praying to see it once more upon a safe return.

The early '70s, not only had muscle cars spitting out globs of pollutants but more cars per capita than ever before. Scanning the skies ten floors above the San Juaquin Valley from Lemoore tower, yellow smog crept north from LA basin. State government began taking drastic action regulating engine pollutants by making catalytic converters mandatory on all cars sold in California.

A couple controllers I knew from work, Dan and Don, were looking for someone to rent a house together in Hanford, around fifteen miles from base. Eight months of living in the barracks flared my old independent streak. Standing in the parking lot at work, we discussed whether Don's current squeeze, Rosie, was included rent free.

"We've been together a couple months, so she's on my tab," Don said, leaning against his Datsun 210.

"We're talking more than drinks on a tab here," Dan replied.

Both looking at me, I said, "No qualms…she's gotta cook better than us."

"I'll ask," Don answered.

We agreed she essentially could take advantage of the situation to maintain her status of what would become a conniving mooch. Social shindigs became the rule rather than the occasional occurrence.

Dan pulled his Datsun pickup onto Highway 198E out of Hanford toward Visalia, gateway to the Sequoia National Forest. Stopping at a gas station, Rosie got out of Don's car following us. "Olympia or Coors?" she posed, walking past the truck. "Olys," we said in unison. Recent qualifications of controllers had allowed the division to utilize a watch bill, allowing three days off in a row. Today's mission—enjoy those days off before the watch bill changes again.

Forty-five minutes or so later, an orange orchard beyond the road's shoulder involuntarily offered up a dozen huge fruits. The foothills just beyond had a breeze adequate to lift our kites as far as our string would allow. Oranges and Olys consumed, we climbed higher up the Sierra Nevada, reaching the day's goal of snow-fed mountain streams—as in jumping in for as long as your body can stand it. We reached the top of huge boulders on the stream's edge below, at least a fifteen-foot drop. Churning clear water flowed passed; white caps created by upstream rapids into the deeper hole directly below. Rosie pushed ahead out onto the business edge of the rock, looked down, turned around, and said, "Who can top this?" Did a backward flip off the boulder, lining up for a pinpoint entry into the frigid water below. Dan and I both looked at Don as if he'd been hiding something we didn't realize existed.

"Did you know she could do that?" I asked.

Goggle-eyed at her dive, Don said, "No idea. She's been holding back on me."

Dan injected, "Maybe a little more physical activity and you'd find out," and he sprinted straight ahead off the boulder.

We charged ahead daily, mesmerized with life, waiting for no one. Upon return from a two weeks' leave in Oregon, Don confronted Rosie's new allegiance to Dan—the stink bomb which could not be fumigated from our unique living arrangement. I was headed back to Lemoore's barracks. "When the levee breaks, momma you've got to move" (Led Zeppelin 1971).

Within a month, Dan and Rosie were busted for distributing pot to a minor. Not exactly the bragging rights the US Navy likes publicized. Of course, Naval Investigative Service promptly interviewed Don and me. We deployed the tight-lip syndrome knowing that loose lips sink ships or, in this case, careers. Dan and Rosie got what they deserved. Barracks' life paled in any comparison, severely curtailing quality time off from work. I was stuck somewhere between David Bowie's "Moonage Daydream" and Cat Stevens' "Cosmic Plain."

On occasion, since 1970, I had smoked pot preferring it over the nagging effects of alcohol. If ushering in a few hours of organic euphoria instead of gut-wrenching drunken spasms from alcohol was illegal, so be it. For me, centuries of use by American Indians proved this natural herb was safe if used, like alcoholic beverages, responsibly with moderation. Despite most misgivings, cannabis is nonaddictive and grown in God's green earth. It had been stigmatized by the self-anointed, morally superior factions and spewed forth from pulpits around the nation prompting restrictive laws, as during prohibition. Whether alcohol or marijuana, some people will abuse them. When available, pot was that "Ticket to Ride" (Beatles, 1965). Granted the navy punished people for this act yet had no standardized urinalysis to thwart its use as of that time. If one was careful and only used it while off duty, the tightwire act was possible.

Bob, a radar controller, played his Ovation guitar with practiced ease emulating his idol, Dave Mason. If he could pry that guitar out of his hands long enough, I suggested we go camping up in Yosemite on our next days off. Bob, lubricated from the speakeasy effects the now-empty wine bottle had produced, implied he could skin his first bear along the way. Weeks later, we selected a campsite on the valley floor, El Capitan looming above us. A dying campfire between our bedrolls, tomorrow's hike was planned.

Campers began screaming from afar replaced by closer screams. If some hatchet-wielding lunatic was on the loose, no blood-thirsty killer was going to rob Bob of any sleep. The closest campsite thirty yards through the woods erupted with the same clamor, indicating we may be next. No club was within grasp from my bedroll. A riding-mower-sized mass of brown hair and white teeth galloped through the moonlight directly toward our bedrolls. The untamed Yosemite spirit of Yogi grubbing a few morsels from more tamed newcomers. Without Boo-Boo, it ran over dying coals between Bob and I, dispensing enough of a gagging odor to finally awaken Bob. So much for any sleep that night; dearly missed the next day climbing El Capitan.

The hurdle I'd worked toward since initially checking into NAS Lemoore was behind me. I gained the tower qualification I'd pursued. The realization of accomplishing something I'd started back in Georgia resulting with a FAA qualification ticket at a master jet base gave my self-confidence some comfort that hard work did pay off. AC1 Armstrong told me, "You've punched your ticket in this tower, you can do it anywhere." The proverbial grains of salt over my shoulder; maybe I was onto something here. Armstrong was a "lifer" though, probably attempting to lure me into the same status. Would never happen—having joined to avoid the draft back in '72, six months from now I'd be rotated to an aircraft carrier counting the days, primed and ready to resume college upon leaving the navy.

As if a bowl, the San Joaquin Valley is nestled between mountain ranges where, in addition to syphoning off water from the Colorado River, it somehow collects enough moisture to raise immense amounts of crops each year. During winter months one would be correct to assume that moisture, now fog, would be prevalent within those mountainous confines. See where this is heading? No, not the massive car wrecks on I-5 during fog-plagued, low-visibility situations. The weather observation, W0X0F, had appeared on the weather screen monitor in the tower the last two hours. Its code meant, "Indefinite Ceiling Zero, Sky Obscured, Visibility Zero due to Fog." Visibility improved enough that aircraft approaches could be made down to their weather minimums for the approach. If the pilot had the runway in sight, a clearance could be issued.

Awaiting response from departure control after requesting an IFR (instrument flight rules) release for a search-and-rescue helicopter heading toward the Three Rivers area, I heard:

"Lemoore Tower, Fresno departure."

"Go ahead."

"Lemoore Search and Rescue Helicopter 059 is released eastbound direct Visalia, BH."

"Roger, call him airborne this time, JH."

From below in the radar room, I hear: "Tower, GCA (ground-controlled approach). Romeo-Whiskey 39, P-3 is on a ten-mile dogleg to final GCA full stop, JA."

"GCA, Tower. Check three miles, JH."

"Tower, GCA. RW39 at three, JA."

"GCA, Tower. Cleared to minimums, JH."

"Tower, GCA. Breaking off, JA."

Visibility was poor to nil in that sector. The P-3 finally came into view, not climbing straight ahead on the runway's heading as it was just previously advised by GCA to do, but in a left climbing turn directly on a collision course with, you guessed it, the control tower.

"RW39, Lemoore Control Tower on guard. Increase rate of climb immediately, control tower at your twelve o'clock and closing." Unkeying the transmitter, my knees began an involuntary crouching motion as the undercarriage of the P-3 approached. Before I could get to tower's internal ladder and jump, the P-3's desperate climb took out a whip antenna extending just above the cab as it passed over within feet, surely avoiding what would have decapitated the tower while demolishing the aircraft.

"GCA, Tower. We're still here…by inches. Gonna mount that pilot's wings on the tower's bulkhead, JH."

Kings River ambled through San Juaquin Valley, flowing under a bridge a few miles away from the base, where a gathering spot for sailors and locals existed. I'd returned late, the night before, from a trip up to Modesto, taking in a concert by Elvin Bishop, an open-air venue at their local football stadium. The loud banging in my head did not sound like what I'd heard at the concert the night before. Finally, I opened the door to my barrack's room. Bob said, "Get dressed, keg at King's River in an hour." With four hours sleep, my head could not fathom why I would want to flop down on a river's sandbar. "It's non-family fun," Bob insisted. "Just the kind your parents told you to stay away from, like the song by Three Dog Night, 'Momma Told Me (Not to Come)' (1967)."

Most people growing up in the US generally have a sense of what's normal versus abnormal, right? That other side of the "most people" coin landed face up on the King's River sandbar that Saturday afternoon. We gathered on a sandy bank totaling maybe a dozen controllers. It was good to blow off steam; guess it could be termed as such. I joined a couple radar controllers on the sandbar throwing frisbee, gradually luring the other guy toward the river's edge. Don walked up with some beers.

An hour maybe into this shindig, two blonde females, approximately our age, sauntered up out of nowhere totally butt naked (abnormal). Now they could have been drunk, stoned, maybe just escaped from some sex addict clinic. How were we to know? They didn't stumble around discombobulated or act off-kilter in any fashion. One thing for sure, the gawk factor from all of us peaked out any register.

Trying to contain the instant onslaught of pheromones, any twenty-year-old male's sexual appetite who wasn't blind would produce; we invited them to sit on the blankets we had on the sand. First guess I had—probably hookers, maybe tired of the spiked hills and miniskirts, now going for the gusto. Nah, their attitude couldn't have been more casual than someone hanging out clothes talking over a fence to a neighbor. They sat across from myself and others on the blanket, Indian style, as if I was a practicing gynecologist. Suddenly, an audience of a dozen controllers gathered behind, tails wagging like a pack of horny dogs, exchanging comments with the bold females. "Are you guys trying to lure out the Golden State Killer on some undercover operation?" Bob threw out.

"Of course not, we're nature lovers."

"Naturally," Bob replied.

Granted, local radio stations had been playing some goofy song lately concerning streaking, yet without a doubt, these two Nordic tarts casually sauntered right up amongst us, not running at all. Now, some may think with twelve sailors on hand, these two women were—I'll let your imagination take over.

Didn't happen. We had a twenty-minute conversation and they left. No gang bang, no one-on-one entanglements. Zip-a-dee-doo-dah, and they were on to their next conversation somewhere down river.

Bob looked at Don. Don looked at me. We all turned, verifying we weren't in some discreet porno movie, as crazy as this all seemed. Finishing his beer, Bob said to no one in particular, "Why didn't anyone make a move on those two?"

I picked up the frisbee and said, "Odds were you'd have a seething case of 'advanced clap' in two days."

"I heard syphilis take years to eat away at your brain?" Bob flatly stated.

"You guys are making excuses," Don countered. "They were hot."

"Group mentality. Had to be...everyone here works with one another. If one of us had asked them to go behind the bushes, the whole division, top brass and down, would have known the next day," I replied.

Heading back to base, Bob said, "Admirable, that's it…right now I'm feeling admirable. Tonight I'm going to kick myself in the ass."

"I'm already there. I can't get those images out of my thoughts," I said. "Tonight, I'll be cussin' group mentality."

"Would you have acted so noble out there alone?"

I started singing an old tune from back in college. "Laying on my back, in the newly mowed grass. Rain coming down…lay down beside me, love ain't for keeping." The Who (1972).

Mondays were for field day—a term the navy introduced to me indicating time to clean spaces. All areas assigned to our division had to be cleaned. The ten-story control tower structure, both the stairwell and elevator up to the tower cab, was on tab. The dicey part involved washing tower windows on the outside then drying them with a long-handled squeegee. Pre-harness requirement days, where leaning back against the waist-high bar was needed to clean the windows, stretching ten feet above. Obviously, enough sailors hadn't fallen backward yet; must be waiting on a certain number before implementing a safety harness requirement. Granted, I'd only had two years of college but come on. From that position, I knew it wouldn't be long before someone paid the ultimate price.

Inside the tower, radio speakers were turned up as controllers were dusting and wiping off radio consoles before Airman Gonzales pulled out the vacuum cleaner. The airport sweeper truck called for access onto Runway 32R for cleaning the last two grand of a ten-thousand-foot runway. Permission was granted as I took out my little toy truck and prominently placed it next to the handheld microphone. This was a crutch for me to remember a "foul deck" was in progress during field days. When all types of information are flowing back and forth, any little reminder that your runway is not clear helps.

The daily flight schedule wasn't commencing for another hour, but a C-123 aircraft on the transient line had power carts attached, indicating a departure was imminent. The C-123 was a two-engine version of the four engine C-130, both of which had been used to dispense Agent Orange over the jungle environment up and down Vietnam's Ho Chi Minh trail. The infinite wisdom of some "top-brass brainard" had deduced that killing vegetation could improve visual access needed to wipe out all the reinforcements southbound along said trail. This decision disregarded the safety of all personnel flying the aircraft during the act of dispensing the agent. This short-sighted decision not only killed virtually every living thing on the ground but personnel in the aircraft as well. Death wasn't as immediate as a lethal booby trap with sharp wooden spikes swinging up from the jungle floor impaling US military personnel, but a drawn-out agonizing episode.

    I told AC2 Donovan, the other qualified controller, that I was going to clean the elevator one deck below. I made him aware the runway was foul pointing toward my miniature truck on the console. While Gonzales squeegeed the outside windows, Donovan wiped down the BRITE II radar display. Ten minutes later, Gonzales began vacuuming the consoles inside the tower, pushing aside my foul-deck reminder. The C-123 called requesting his IFR clearance to Moffett Field in San Francisco. Donovan signaled Gonzales to temporarily halt the vacuum. Clearance issued, Donovan taxied the outbound C-123 to 32R. Engine run-up in progress, the outbound aircraft held short. Gonzales vacuumed once again.

    I finish the elevator field day then stopped by the head before returning up the one flight of stairs to the tower. Hearing the engine turnup in progress, I knew Donovan must have the aircraft in the warm-up area at the approach end of the runway.

    "Lemoore tower, JUGG33 for departure," the C-123 called as AC2 Donovan signaled a halt to the vacuum once more. Donovan walked across the tower cab, advised JUGG33 to hold short while coordinating a release from Fresno Departure. Climbing the final ladder up into the tower cab, I heard, "JUGG33, wind 300 at 10, change to departure control, cleared for takeoff."

    Now at tower level, I saw Gonzales holding his vacuum hose. Donovan was writing a departure time down on a flight strip which had JUGG33's callsign on it. Force of habit made me visually scan the length of the runway ahead of JUGG33's pending departure.

"Donovan, the runway is foul," I said! Near the departure end of the runway, although eight thousand feet apart, the sweeper was chugging along the runway centerline, unknowingly playing chicken with a departing C-123.

Donovan picked up the microphone advising, "JUGG33 on guard, departure clearance cancelled, hold in position." Fortunately, the pilot was monitoring the guard channel. Tower had effed up big-time! Lessons were learned. New procedures were implemented during field day. US Navy keeps a tidy ship.

Senior Chief Briggs called me down from the tower into his office. I'd worked for him as office secretary for a couple months awaiting my position in line to begin training. "Who do you know in Washington DC?" Senior Chief inquired. Knowing his sense of humor, I just waited to see where he was going with this. "Harper, you just struck gold." No idea how to respond, I waited while other chiefs in the office gathered. Senior Chief continued, "In my long career I, along with thousands of other sailors, would've walked the plank for what you're getting." He said my orders for sea duty would be spent not on a ship but at Cubi Point Naval Air Station in Subic Bay, Philippines, where a navy-ran airport similar to Lemoore was located adjacent a ship repair facility. The isolated location around the globe in Southeast Asia counted to the navy as sea duty.

Never having heard of the place, I stood amazed, realizing that I had sea duty but at an airport. Everyone congratulated me as if I'd won the lottery—going to a sailor's paradise! Most sought-after duty. Most available women in one port, worldwide. A favorite R & R site in SE Asia for US military-wide in the last ten years. The luck of completing a four-year tour in the navy without having to even set foot on a ship was beginning to swell my head—phantom stories of sea duty were dime a dozen, rampant in sailor's woes. The impending tidal wave of females slowly manifested. Rod Stewart had so aptly put, "Hadn't been getting enough of what keeps a young man alive." (1971)

Naval Air Station Cubi Point, Subic Bay, Philippines—September 1975

Trans World Airlines' seventeen-hour flight time to the other side of the world—San Francisco to Clark AFB, Philippines—still required a fifty-mile trek via bus toward the coast. Climate resembled oppressive humidity from swamps and bayous back home.

Adjacent to Subic Bay Ship Repair, Cubi Point Naval Air Station's airport had been carved out of the side of a mountain by Navy Seabees. Jutting out into Subic Bay's waters on three sides, it was designed to support the squadrons off each aircraft carrier heading into Subic for repairs or ship's liberty, not unusual for two carriers in port at a time. The intensity of air traffic was equal to Lemoore's. Cubi Point had only one runway—the hurdle. A simple 8,000-foot runway yet—extremely valuable property—so many simultaneously wanting its usage. Exactly the scenario I was hoping to find and learn from.

In addition to normal traffic, a nightmare scenario, occurring one day prior to each aircraft carrier's arrival into Subic, was called a CAG inbound. Basically, a carrier's air group sends all available aircraft off ship, in mass, before entering port. Arriving at Cubi Point the same way, skies around the airport resembled bees around a hive, each wanting priority to land. This job would prove my metal or send me packing. Each time an air traffic controller switches duty stations, they begin training anew at each control position, learning the local terrain, and specific capabilities at each new airport.

Unlike the murky, gray waters of the Gulf of Mexico, blue waves, washing onto sandy beaches surrounded by mountains covered with green jungle vegetation, were equally as striking as San

Francisco's allure yet remotely exotic. Barracks' roommate AC1 Billy Ellinder said as we jumped onto a jeepney heading out to the barrio for a bite, "Thirty years since the Jap navy controlled this area. Now, Marcos has the whole country under martial law, including a midnight to dawn curfew. Outside the base, Philippines' customs and laws gotta be respected. Philippine Constabulary will get you. They hang out in groups of two. You see 'em, steer clear."

By this time, I was engorged in the prawns he'd ordered for us sitting at a table over the water they came out of. "You'll get two weeks orientation from the navy to settle you in to this environment. Give you some insight about how to keep from getting your throat cut out in town. *Listen* if you want to survive. The number that hasn't would surprise you. Harper, the thing is…takes a couple weeks for most sailors or marines to realize the balance of need between the local community and the US military. Our greenbacks for their services. Granted, no doubt what sailors need…we're not angels on some spiritual retreat here at the jungles' edge. Most of us become hypnotized at the beauty of the area and the people. Learn to appreciate it."

While training on flight data position in the tower, a regular office phone rang next to the control console where I was working. At the time, multiple aircraft were requesting flight clearances which I was processing. After a few rings, I picked up the phone and couldn't understand the broken English some Filipino was talking about. Quite busy, I entertained for about two seconds how some Filipino was able to call the tower on an in-house line anyway. I advised the person to standby, then put the phone down on the counter. "Cubi Point flight data, November Juliet 011 is awaiting IFR clearance to Taipei," the pilot requested through my headset.

"November Juliet 011 clearance on request with Manila center, standby," I replied.

A couple minutes later, the tower supervisor asked who was holding on the phone. Still busy at flight data, I told him, "Some fuckin' Flip." His eyes got bigger than Marty Feldman's. Operations Department Master Chief, a Filipino in the US Navy, was still holding (unfortunate for me, also still listening) on the line and wanting my butt in front of his desk immediately. So went my introduction to respecting the local people and their customs. I learned fast.

Olongapo, the town outside the base, bustled with activity from sunrise to curfew at midnight, supporting locals with open-air markets of fresh seafood and meat without that "expensive refrigeration." Ah, yes, that arousing aroma. US dollars, flowing freely from American pockets, lured the best musicians from Manila for off-base nightclubs. After sundown, door to door clubs such as the New Florida Club or the Astro Club began cranking up with a few musicians comparable to stateside—Rick, the guitarist at the Astro Club for example. Bar hopping was entertainment too good to pass up, whether rock 'n' roll or disco. These clubs had young women hoping to make a few pesos if a sailor or marine bought them a watered-down drink. Caught up in the good times, many sailors believed these women were just as full of gusto as they were; not pausing to think this was their method of income, many supporting their parents and children back in their barrio.

Larry, a friend from the barracks, and I finally made it up one side of Magsaysay (the main drag) polishing off a San Miguel beer at every fifth bar. Magsaysay Street started at the bridge over "shit-river," outside the main gate, where vendors plied everything from roasted "monkey on a stick" to "Imelda Marcos' gallstone" guaranteed (how, I don't know). Gin palaces, massage parlors, sari-sari stores, *pandesal* bakeries (good for hangovers), an occasional café inter-mixed between, but mostly nightclubs. Each club had their own version of a house band, ranging from god-awful to excellent musicians with mild accents.

Larry and I edged our way through sailors and marines gawking up at the go-go dancers on the stage at the New Florida Club. The place packed, as each of the four times I'd been there, bartenders mixed Mojo and popped the top on San Miguel beers, keeping the pace with the music's beat. One of the better, if not loudest bar bands playing, of all things, Leonard Skinner's "Free Bird" (1974). Despite the excellent original guitar work by Skinner, I'd avoided the song after an old high-school flame had referenced the song's title as her view of our relationship.

"What's wrong, San Miguel curdling your supper?" Larry asked, leaning against the bar.

"Hell, there's no alternative. Mojo would guarantee I got carried out of here on a stretcher," I replied, not wanting to get into the song-ruining whims of an ex-girlfriend. Gigi Baviera, a hostess I'd went home with a few nights before, approached.

My inner alarm clock woke me prior to sunrise, from only a few hours of sleep. Departing Gigi's meager abode for the navy base's main gate, I wound through the alley discovering I was surrounded by four Filipino men. Possessing no weapon other than uncultivated wits a mere twenty-one-year-old my limited background could possibly have, I was knee deep in hot water.

They pushed me into an open doorway of some abandoned residence. Heart rate maxed out; anxiety launching brilliant flares; looking for some way out of this. The one-night stand I'd just consummated had left my wallet with minimal funds. In no way were these guys going to be happy finding that out. My problem, understanding these guys' attempt at English, didn't help in an already dicey situation. My concentration centered on how far they were willing to go to get anything of value off me.

The guy spitting out unintelligible demands had a sadistic smile. The pleasure of turning that face to Jello with my fist occupied one too many seconds as I pondered my plight. The butterfly knives under a couple of their belts indicated where this whole scene could end for me—my secret identity, unfortunately, was not Bruce Lee. Used as a table within this structure, an old box crate sat off to one side with, of all things, a deck of cards. Their pastime, waiting for their next victim, I guess.

I placed a smile on my solemn face, pointed at the cards, and challenged this guy doing the blabbering to cut the cards. "I win, I walk." If I lose well, who knew? Instantly, his expression changed. His eyes darted from my face to his cohorts; his understanding of my version of English apparently easier attained than his in my ears. This move offset the dynamics among the four thugs. They must have expected all challenges would be a one-way street in my direction. I'm no shrink, but I'd thrown a monkey wrench into their standard operating procedure.

He forced a smile under the rattiest attempt of a mustache I'd honestly ever seen—a criticism I kept to myself. We slowly moved toward the crate. If I chanced bargaining more, they'd want to see what my wallet contained—maybe five pesos. My hope was to take the fifty-fifty chance of winning the cut. If successful, I'll use any such luck discreetly exiting, presumptuous of walking out after a win. I gestured him to go first. He shuffled the lymph deck, their firmness completely erased from overuse. Drawing out a ten of clubs, he composed a smile of victory, knowing the odds. Damn, fate had me by the balls, shrinking as the seconds ticked away. Reaching for the grungy deck, time seemed suspended. My hand's movement slowed; my mind raced. If this goes south, butterfly knives or not, I'd decided to make a dash for it.

Jack of spades appeared in my hand. No word uttered, no cracked smile; not even the desired "up yours" gesture. Fate was in the balance; I was walking straight out the door, with no looking back. Five steps in, senses maxed out, my body's defensive mechanisms primed by any measurement; I reached the alleyway. Turning toward the base, the rising sun hit my eyes before any semblance of hope ignited. Crossing the "shit river" bridge toward the main gate, my thoughts lingered on a song I'd heard last night by the Allman Brothers called "One Way Out" (1972). Mental note: change underwear before going to work.

Tower supervisor on duty, turned airport lighting on low since it was sunset. The green and white rotating beacon revolved from an elevated platform on the airport. The civilian, transit aircraft, with prior permission, landed at runway 07. I directed it to base operations where some dignitaries were awaiting its arrival. Base Ops had passed along a VIP (very important person) was onboard.

For now, no traffic was flying. PO2 Sager, the tower supervisor, said, "Harper, I'm going to clean your clock in gin rummy."

Base Ops called the tower and asked, "Can you get a look at her?"

"Who?"

"The VIP, it's Gina Lollobrigida."

Instantly with binoculars in hand, we popped tall to see the 1960s Italian bombshell, famous for once being called "the sexiest woman alive." Our appraisal of that claim was dashed by the diminishing light available. Base Ops stated she was being picked up by President Marcos' private car. Sager stated, "Imelda must be out of town."

"Look across the bay at the hill beyond Olongapo," I said looking through a set of binoculars. "That's the cemetery along the road to Barrio Barreta where I live." A good three miles as the crow flies; many handheld lanterns were slowly moving along the hillside; eerie and odd, the whole scene a strange sight from a distance. "What the hell are they doing out there at night?"

Sager picked up another set of binoculars. "It's All Saints' Day, Filipinos clean their dead relatives' graves during the night and celebrate their past loved ones. Back home, it's Halloween, here it's different. Harper, I heard you had to go to XO's mast, what'd you do?"

"Marine guard at the front gate determined I didn't have the correct license to drive out in town. I've been going back and forth on the cycle for over a month through that gate, no problems. This guard picked the day I had fresh meat from the commissary on board and needed to get it home before it went bad. We went back and forth until he gave me a direct order to turn around and remain on the base. I turned around but drove to the back gate in hopes of an exit there. They were waiting for me due to a heads up from the front gate to be on the lookout. Security was waiting for me as I rode right up to them. Wrote me up, disobeying a direct order."

"How did you not know about the required license for off base?"

"I knew...just put off getting it."

"Did the XO bust you?"

"I pleaded ignorant. Senior Chief Pelagrim stood up for me which I was grateful for. XO told me to write an essay on all the licenses required for driving here and give it to senior chief. That's it, I got lucky."

"Senior chief already knows you, and Hoag were marching on the ramp two weeks ago. Did he ask you about that?"

"Yeah, I told him the truth. During division fall in on the ramp, we were at parade rest. Cubi Point's C-117 taxied to its line, parking about fifty yards away. AC1 Flint, our section leader in formation behind Hoag and myself, determined the forty-five-degree angle our head turned observing the shutdown was too much for him to take. He yanked us aside afterward, spewing his wrath, essentially telling Hoag and myself to report to AC3 Bohannon the next morning. In front of base operations with aircraft taxiing by for all to see, Bohannon, who we're senior to, called 'close order drill.' Hoag says Flint hates him for color of his skin…claims that is what this is all about. I'm included to make it less obvious."

"Did you tell senior chief that?"

"Hoag didn't want it to get back to Flint. No telling what Flint is capable of."

I'd learned something interesting about Hoag and asked him the next morning after muster. "Did you grow up in the Frisco area?"

"Yeah, dude. What's it to you?" Hoag replied.

"I just left the area before getting here. I've felt lately there's something to that song about leaving a part of you in San Francisco…don't know how much, maybe a chunk of funk. I will return to reclaim it though. What say you? Will you be returning?"

"Not anytime soon. Look, I love the bay area…grew up on the docks of Oakland where Otis sang his last song before he became a victim of aviation. Snuck away for a week the summer of my sophomore year hanging out around Haight Asbury. Seen the craziest shit ain't ever seen before."

"Wait, you were on the streets of San Francisco in Haight Ashbury summer of '67?"

"I'm not playing echo here," Hoag reminded me.

"Okay, okay…what was it like on the street or where they gathered?" I asked, having heard different versions.

"Was going on sixteen…had to find out what all the buzz the past month was about. Told my mom I was going camping, took off. From the beginning, my race forgot to show up, mostly whites except for a few like me. Mushrooms were all you needed. Any kind of substance, natural or man-made, was free. Sex was free. A bunch of boogaloo dudes with some new music. All kind of free food. Hippie lifestyle, with that peace and love bullshit. I'd never been to anything like it."

"Hoag, what turned you against the place?"

"San Francisco 'heat.' They 'made' my first cousin as a member of the SLA (Symbionese Liberational Army) after they had already killed him. Started prying into my past, where I didn't want any one's nose sniffing. Volunteered at the recruitment office, and here I am marching around some ramp to the tune of old, white-dude, mofos."

"Is he after your ass? Flint, I mean."

"Ain't it clear? I questioned, to his face, why I'm the only person he calls when someone else forgets to make a new pot of coffee. He doesn't like confrontation, especially if that person is my skin color. Harper, that SOB can kiss my ass. Purple Haze bar, 6:00 p.m. this evening, be there, the more Mojo the merrier."

Imagine, if you will, driving your vehicle into some metropolitan US city, for example, Houston or Atlanta, around 4:00 p.m. Bumper to bumper traffic with probably six to eight lanes each side of the median. Music playing or the driver's thoughts away on some beach—traffic regulations, ingrained from the age of fifteen into our psyche, take over. Before you know it, you're home. Now remove the median; forsake the marked lanes; forget about speed zone enforcement; hell, there's no speed limit anyway; no right side or left side traffic. You're in the YOYO zone (You're on Your Own). Welcome to the highways and byways of the Philippines (per '75.) This situation wasn't restricted just to smaller towns and villages but existed in and around the capital city of Manila. All over the country, streets and roads are ruled by trikes (small motorcycles with a side car), jeepneys (modified jeep to accommodate paying passengers), and large red passenger buses (the king of the road), Victory Liners, for extended travel. This is your competition if you dare to drive a personal vehicle down any road.

I'd witnessed, so far, two collisions with fatalities since arriving. Like those old episodes on Saturdays on ABC's *Wide World of Sports* (mid '60s) featuring bumper-car free-for-alls called demolition derbies. Here, it's *live* every day. No room for the leisurely drive, cruising the curb, maybe a drive wind-down stress—it's Indi-500 on steroids. Larry said, "Jeepney and trike drivers see only centavos and pesos.

Safety is no concern." My sentiments exactly. To avoid putting my life in the hands of a stranger in this scenario, I bought a Honda 550 cc motorcycle as soon as I could. Granted, I'd bought my first back in California, hence, my experience was mediocre. CHIPS, however, was there keeping sanity along Highway 1, from the coast eastward, somewhat in check. Here in the PI, my skills on the crotch-rocket improved, something akin to natural selection, survival of the fittest, or becoming one with the road—take your pick.

Occasionally, a cross-country trip using a Victory Liner was necessary. Here in the PI, prominence of mountainous terrain was obviously conquered on a stiff budget, narrowing what should have remained a two-lane roadway down to one. The king of the road was dominate on these mountainous, curved roads, winding up then down the precarious slopes. Infrequently on these lethal endeavors, passage around these slopes gave proof these road kings were not immune to gravity, as in plunging over the mountainside to a fiery death below. My last trip on a Victory Liner, returning from a visit to a province eight hours south of Manila, passed two such separate crashes.

Whether it be a need for speed; wrapped-up angst needing an airing; or the joy of operating a vehicle free of restrictions; the thrill I experienced jumping from regulated traffic stateside into PI's wild-west road fest was as if your favorite high-velocity, amusement-park ride back stateside, never had a line to wait in. Yes, I admit it, thrill-seeker since a kid; I loved demolition derbies.

Closest call while driving came one morning on my way to work from an off-base bungalow I was renting. No shoulder existed along the narrow road winding along the mountainside; a hundred-foot sheer drop over the cliff into Subic Bay, taking its place. Banking my cycle in the turn, this was now a daily trip for me. I could say I was going less than the speed limit but, you guessed it, there was no limit. I knew it, and I'm certain the driver's eyes, rapidly approaching with a big, red Victory Liner all around them, knew it as well. Bus driver's face had the same localized version of the snarl Jack Nicholson was sporting on the poster for *One Flew Over the Cuckoo's Nest* (1975), I'd been planning to see at a theatre in Olongapo.

Amazing how details, in a snippet of time, get branded on one's memory. Vividly, my recall times-out road hog's closing distance at five seconds, first couple of which were wasted on the driver in an eye lock. His sat atop a wicked grin-from-hell, where, yes, I'd swear on my mother's name, Alice Harper, he was trying to send me. Remaining seconds consisted of a shrinking space between the Victory Liner's exterior side and the jagged precipice, no more than three feet to my right. "Living on the Edge" by Aerosmith (1993). If it was possible for the sphincter muscle to have sneezed, at that point, the outcome would have been hellacious. This mortal coil came as close within those few seconds, to finding what level of existence is next. So went road traffic in the Philippines.

The warm, sunny day occurring just outside the tower windows had a steady flow of local jet traffic sequenced into a long line of straight-in radar-controlled aircraft, specifically a P-3, C-130, and an Air Force C-141. A standard minimum distance of three miles separating the radar straight ins, I cleared the quite faster F-4 Phantom jet in tower's local pattern at base leg. "November Delta 611 in front of C-130, at four miles on a GCA final, wind 140 at 8, check wheels down, cleared touch-and-go."

"Roger."

Tower, Radar on intercom: "C-141, ten-mile dogleg to final has a hydraulic failure with no nose wheel steering capability, declaring an emergency, fourteen souls on board."

"Roger, ringing the bells…C-130 at three miles cleared to land, JH."

"Hellcat71, Cubi Tower, one-mile upwind turn crosswind to follow the GCA traffic."

"Radar, Tower. Your C-141 will close the runway temporarily, what's the P-3s intention and fuel state? I've got an F-4 to get on deck before runway closes, JH."

"Tower, Radar. P-3 is touch-and-go at six miles…fuel state: plenty, OB."

"Radar, Tower. Breakoff the P-3 approach, tower is landing an F-4 in front of the emergency, JH."

"Hellcat71, enter a right base, plan on a full stop, emergency C-141, nine mile straight in, runway closure pending, traffic P-3, five mile straight in is climbing runway heading, wind 140 at 8, check wheels down cleared to land."

"Cubi Tower, Hellcat71, roger, turning crosswind just back there I was low enough to see a substantial shadow approaching sailors in the water at Dungaree Beach."

"Hellcat71…uh, roger. No delay on rollout, expedite clearing the runway."

"Tower, Radar. Three-mile GCA final, C-141, emergency OB."

"Radar, Tower. F-4 clearing runway at three-quarter field, cleared to land JH."

"Tower Supervisor, call over to Dungaree Beach, just received an ariel report of a large shadow, possible shark, in vicinity of observed swimmers. Reported by the F-4."

"You're bullshittin'."

"Tower Supervisor, runway is closed, C-141 no nose-wheel steering…advise the office and *no*, I'm not bullshittin'."

The upwind to crosswind leg in the flight pattern had put the F-4 in a position to see what turned out to be a twelve-to-thirteen-foot Great White shark apparently zeroing in on some fresh meat, as in enlisted sailors getting some well-deserved R & R at the on-base recreational swimming area called Dungaree Beach.

Leaving the airport that afternoon, I began to understand the feeling that had been percolating within some corridor of my brain, its intensity rising. After eight hours, I was getting off from work but thinking of returning to it tomorrow. An air traffic controller on his game can moderate the intensity of situations using their hard-won technique of sequencing, rule application, knowledge of aircraft ability, and control diversity to get the job done. Addicted—in my bloodstream—I was hooked.

AC1 Ellinder, Ed, Larry, and I played a final hand of spades in the barracks. Larry said, "*Stars and* Stripes (overseas military newspaper) mentioned an upcoming Vietnam war movie production team was filming some scenes down south of Manila." It made sense that jungle scenes would be filmed here in the PI instead of war-torn Vietnam. "We ought to check it out, maybe watch how they stage the battle," he said. "My friend in the aeroclub could fly us to Manila where we could jump on a bus to Pagsanjan Falls."

Within a week, Larry and I were in our fourth hour of a bus trip through jungle terrain when the driver pulled to the side of the road. The only Americans onboard, we preferred the rear seats which is where the driver now approached in the narrow aisle. In a broken version of Tagalog-English lingo, he explained that a mile ahead is a checkpoint ran by a Muslim terrorist group called the MPA. Instantly, two American backbones came to "atten-hut." We'd been warned during local indoctrination to avoid such areas. Yet here we sat, surrounded by impenetrable jungle with no weapons—the definition of SOL. The driver was in on it, obviously. Kidnapping for ransom, rape, torture, murder, everything was on the table from the warnings we'd received months before. The driver indicated he knew a friend at the checkpoint who would let us pass through for all our money.

As vulnerable as we felt at that moment, I'm wondering why this guy pulled over a mile from the point. He's the one mighty vulnerable right now, the way I see it; every fiber of me wants to turn this guy to mincemeat pie. Then I recognize his backups in the seats, on both sides, in front of us. "Do it and we'll be on the evening news tonight. Two sailors missing, never to be found again," Larry said in a low whisper.

"We're surrounded here," I mumbled, amazed he'd read my mind.

"Let's play this through…give 'em what they want. We may get out of this alive," Larry suggested.

"It worked for me last month in Olongapo, just keep a cool head," I whispered.

The driver, hearing what we'd just discussed said, "You play cool, you walk away."

"All right, let's get this over with," I grumbled.

Filipinos with old weapons trained in our direction waited as the driver talked to one at the checkpoint. "Empty your pockets" one said. We did. Money, ID cards, Larry's camera. They pointed toward a trike driver on the road's shoulder as our bus pulled away, abandoning us.

Larry and I look at each other. "Is playing the cool part over with yet? Wanted to pull a Bronson on that bus-driving bastard so bad," I moaned in his direction. "Is this 'trikester' here to help us?" We approached the trike, asking for a lift somewhere, anywhere. No mention was made of payment because this SOB had watched us get shaken down and ripped off.

"He's paid up, get in already," Larry sneered lunging into the sidecar. I squeezed onboard what little part of my body would fit into the passenger compartment. We were off, putt-putting down an isolated road in a jungle on our way to a damned river in some friggin' movie. We still weren't out of this. Leery of our suspicions, the driver sped down this road through the jungle for around ten minutes before dropping us off—where else but the village of Pagsanjan.

I'm as completely frazzled as a down and out, ransacked and ripped off, unidentifiable and completely broke sailor, five hours somewhere south of Manila through thick and deadly jungle, could understandably be. Larry is chirping along the roadside as if he'd just eaten a mango slushie. "Larry, what kind of sunbeam acid are you taking? We're in deep do-do here. Can't you act like it? At least cuss out that bus driver or something."

"You're sweating enough for us both. This is where we were heading, so at least we've made it. There should be members of the film crew hanging around if needed."

"An inconvenient bump in the road, was it? Psyched-out thieves pretending to be political, stand-for-somethings, holding live weapons on us...just, no peskier than mosquitos to you, I guess. We gotta get an idea of how many of these idiots are around us. It's going to be hard enough managing reentry to the base without an ID, but we're broke...way out here," I said, lifting my arms to the sky.

He smiled my way during a 360-degree spin of his body, surveilling the immediate area. "We get to the river, check in to a bungalow, buy some coconut wine, and relax." Before I could erupt, he ran his fingers along his belt from navel to hip.

I looked around myself now. "Is what's in there, what I'm thinking's in there?"

Up to that point, Larry wasn't known for smiling, but he placed a doosy below his hairy lip right then.

Film crew for *Apocalypse Now* (1979) had wrapped up two days prior. They had also reported armed thieves in the area. Larry paid for our *banka* boat trip up to Pagsanjan Falls—stunning waterfall with "land of the lost" jungle 360-degrees for a lifetime if walking out. The ends of the earth couldn't have produced a more out-of-the-way locale for a movie set. At least, I notched my guard down, enough to relax after looking down the business end of multiple loaded weapons.

Besides riding backseat into a lethal rip-off, dodging being kidnapped or murdered by the seat of our pants; losing our military ID in a foreign country; and missing out on the whole reason for the trip to begin with; we had enough pesos to reach base and begin the report to authorities.

Larry on his dirt bike, and myself down-shifting the Japanese rice burner I'd had a few months, we rolled into the Buzzard's parking lot hopefully for a few semi-cold ones. Considering our recent misadventure, warm beer never went down as smooth. We'd agreed to not talk of our close call at our individual places of work. If security spread the word, we'd deal with the questions at that point. Larry said, "I met a gorgeous lady name Kristi at the enlisted men's club on-base three weeks ago and tonight is our third date."

"Good for you. Out of the thousands available to choose from, beauty narrows the margin considerably. Now, from that reduced number, if one comes along who's accent you can handle during conversation, you've got a potential keeper?"

"You mentioned on the way to Pagsanjan Falls you'd been seeing Sita. How's her lingo?"

"Her accent is no problem, her mother sent her to a Catholic boarding school where they spoke only English."

Within a week, Larry and I were cruising the curb, hitting every seventh club and enjoying the view walking directly behind Kristi and Sita up ahead. They'd hit it off since meeting a couple hours earlier before pizza.

"Larry, where'd you get that belt that saved our asses last month?"

"It was my dad's. Fighting Rommel in North Africa, he went on liberty in Algiers. Two hoodlums stole all his money. He saved enough doe by the next time liberty occurred. Found a merchant who could make what he wanted. I'm wearing what he bought that night. It served him and, as you know, us well ever since. He made sure I had it before I left to come over here."

"Next time you talk to…WTF." My wallet was being lifted out of my back pocket. I spun around quick enough to catch a miniature pickpocket with his hand on my ass, more specifically my pocketbook. Surely no more than twelve years old, he resembled the fools jumping in shit river for pesos thrown by sailors because his hair was orange. I grabbed his wrist in an iron lock as fast as he was pulling away. Big, wide, racoon-looking eyes returned my gaze. Going nowhere in my grasp, he watched as I calmly took my wallet back out of his hand returned it to my back pocket, then slapped him upside the face with the palm of my hand. When I loosened his wrist—Filipino lightning.

Larry grabbed my shoulder, spun me around and we caught up with the ladies. The whole evolution lasted no more than thirty seconds. "Thank your lucky stars the PC didn't see what you did. You'd been the one arrested."

"Come on…he was the one ripping me off," I scoffed back. "I had witnesses."

"I'm telling you plain and simple, I saw it happen six months ago. PC showed up after a conflict that some local caused. The marine was taken away by the PC. No telling what they did to that guy in their custody. Unless you want that treatment, control your temper around these hoodlums."

The four of us climbed the stairs to the second floor of Astro Club, where the best Filipino guitar player, at least in Olongapo, rendered credit to his race every night. The guy knew his way up and down the frets. Playing Jimi Hendrix's version of "All Along the Watchtower" (1968) written by Bob Dylan, Rick drew customers in off the street—open windows blasting guitar licks at least two blocks away.

In between stints on the dance floor, we sat next to a table of marines who were off the helicopter carrier docked in the bay. Somewhat like the navy's carriers with fixed wing aircraft, marines operate essentially a floating platform ship for rotor wing aircraft. A gunny sergeant named Birdwell introduced himself as I bought the three grunts in uniform a round of San Miguel. Birdwell had joined the marines ten years ago at seventeen out of Paducah and never returned. After three back-to-back tours in Vietnam, he began cross decking from one ship to another to stay in the combat arena.

"Where did you serve in Nam?" Larry asked.

"Unit, mostly in the highlands, chasing tunnel rats," gunny said before finishing his beer.

I quickly ordered another round to keep this guy's story flowing. "Did you get training for that or jump in (no pun intended) cold feet?"

"One day just out of boot camp, volunteers were requested for training in an up-close form of combat unit. I volunteered on the spot. Soon as I got in country, the squad acclimated for two weeks then dove into the fire. Entry into an enemy's tunnel was best served with two brave souls…one leading, one assisting. My first four entries were assist. I've led since."

Processing what I'd just heard, I could tell Birdwell was mentally back in his zone; eyes looking beyond the walls of this club. "Miss, another round for these two tables."

Larry stated, "Can't wrap my head around those first five seconds, after you've jumped in, nightmares I had as a kid…cold sweats. Your eyes aren't adjusted, just too vulnerable.

I felt the fifth San Miguel I was a quarter into, but the gunny may as well have been drinking lemonade.

"Forty-five, flashlight, and a Bowie…anything else weighed me down. Mobility's the key," Birdwell sang.

"Cojones the size of coconuts must not have slowed you down," I said raising the bottle of San Miguel in salute; everyone at the two tables joining in.

"Is it too personal to ask, how many kills you've had?" Larry brought up, too personal or not.

"That's not a number you'll ever hear from my lips. Each one died a 'good death.' I could've easily been lying beside them." Gunny sighed.

"Karma!" Larry declared, feeling his sixth.

Finishing his seventh beer, Gunny Sergeant looked like he'd just walked in. On his neck below his right ear was a unique tattoo of a skeleton, bowie knife held between the skull's teeth, crawling through a tunnel. On that number of kills, Birdwell brought up, as if he'd been counting them, "More than graduated Paducah High School 1965."

"Look, Gunny Sergeant Birdwell, before we break up this truce between the two rival factions of the naval department, tell me, what is the most harrowing experience you will still remember when you're seventy years old?" I asked, wondering if this was my sixth or seventh of the PI's only cerveza.

Birdwell took a long drag off the San Miguel, darn near wiped it out. His eyes took on that familiar gaze once more, as if he'd just dropped down the shaft into a "hot" tunnel. "We were on the third day out, canvassing mountainous terrain when a secluded 'cave' opening was found. Small, but I'd squeezed through half that before. This was a natural opening but still needed to be checked out. I had no one to assist as my back up, but that happened half the time anyway. Added some rope to my belt just in case. Who knows the drop-off there could be in an actual cave? Able to stand at fifteen feet within the cave, visibility was waning…I could feel it, something with me… close, couldn't see it yet, but I sensed 'em. I froze, listened…"

As if I stood there in the cave behind the sergeant, I found myself prone and ready to attack, actually holding my breath and waiting for his next word. If there was ever a time I wanted a joint, it was right then.

Birdwell continued. "A corridor branched off immediately to the right leading to complete darkness. It was from there, it turned to face me. No more than five feet in front of me, enough natural light shown on a man-sized lizard standing upright…my height. Its eyes locked upon mine, blinking as would a man's. Its lower extremities resembled human legs, covered with the scales of a serpent, a long tail behind. My forty-five remained pointed downward, I made no movement...just observed, as did it. Whatever this was, there was intelligence coming out of those eyes. A good minute into this stare down, it returned to its cloak of darkness. I make a one-eighty exit myself. 'Cave's clear!' I yelled, exiting the entrance, eyes glaring out the back of my head. Didn't sleep for a week, which nearly got me killed due to the jitters. I've never really been the same since."

Severe slack jaw for me, had set up back when the gunny was in a stare down with the life-size gecko from down under. This guy was stone-cold serious. No bloodshot eyes; clear as the seven seas. The three grunts shook our hands, got up, and headed back to their ship, thanking us for the rounds of San Miguel.

"You're going to have to tell me tomorrow if what I think I heard tonight is what I really heard," Larry said in my direction, as all four of us headed down the stairs to Magsaysay then on to the next nightclub.

Sita, the Filipina I'd been seeing, along with her two young children, moved with me into a bungalow. It sat adjacent an elevated bluff above the sandy beaches in Barrio Barreta within Subic Bay. Back in the states, a sailor of my rank, then E-5, barely scraped by on the US economy, whereas in the Philippines, we were rich compared to most. Clothes, be it uniform or civilian, hung to dry just outside the back door, would go missing; a new motorcycle, only outside my bedroom window, had to be chained to the wall; a new maid stole over two hundred dollars one morning as she took out the trash never to return—all, obviously in dire straits, these people reeked of desperation beginning with nothing and exactly that to lose.

Statistics seem to apply to others, don't they? Since arrival in country, I was constantly harped upon by the USN against marrying Filipina women. Didn't bother me; never figured I would become part of that statistic. Reflections from a setting sun bathed the beach at Barrio Barreta; "Seagull" by Bad Company (1974) serenaded the air as played by Fred Miles Watson on US Armed Forces Radio; my "crossroads" moment ignited. Could I leave my love interest behind when I left the PI? If I had to, yes. Could I leave her kids behind? Absolutely not!

Any visitor in a third-world country, witnessing the starkest poverty imaginable, must decide to help in some way or let it slide. For three years, all pistons had been firing within me to return to college after this four-year enlistment; however, I'd found a marketable trade for the future whether in or out of the military. Now, in a position to do something that would payoff for their future, I had only minimal time available to complete the mountain of paperwork before my departure date—a time crunch. Deliberations had no room; it was decision time.

True colors of once-close friends vividly labeling me, not only a fool for marrying a local but with two kids as well, was stark. Clearly others could walk away, yet opportunity was what these kids deserved. Regardless, proof of support, as in an awaiting job, was required to get the family into the US. Bada bing, bada boom! They had me. Reenlistment for another four years would be necessary. We married August 9, '76.

Eicher and Vanzetti, two younger sailors, arrived for duty. Their experience with air traffic control was gleaned from school only. Eager to learn, they had to wait their turn. Ed and I warned them of areas out in town where bars ripped off drunk sailors. We mentioned that Subic City (sin city) was dangerous and not to go there alone. Good pals, Eicher and Vanzetti had been through air traffic control school together then got orders to the same base.

The day watch was over, and Vanzetti, in my section, had been given study guides for position training on flight data. Eicher met Vanzetti at the barracks with the proposal of hitting Olongapo for a night out. "Give me one hour for some study and I'll go," Vanzetti replied.

The rendezvous was set at the Purple Haze Bar on Magsaysay Boulevard. By the time Vanzetti arrived a little late, Eicher was two sails into the wind, working on a third. They both began a slow curbside cruise. Vanzetti caught up with Eicher's inebriated state after two glasses of Mojo. Eicher, tipsy no doubt, stated, "Zetti, it's been a year since I touched a woman but tonight's the night."

"Do you see who's all around us? Thicker than flies, just reach out and touch one…problem solved."

"Let's go to Subic City."

"We're practically drowning in females right here, pick one."

"All that routine of buying the hostess out of the club for the night, I'm not familiar with yet." Can't understand 'em…so talking's out. I was thinking wham, bam, see ya later."

"Harper said Subic City was dangerous."

Eicher grabbed Vanzetti by the arm and led him to an empty jeepney. "Let's rent this jalopy."

"Whatever amount he charges, tell him you'll only pay half of it. If he doesn't like it, go to the next driver."

Passing the outskirts of Barrio Barreta, Vanzetti told the driver to stop at the Buzzard Inn, a biker bar (sailors with motorcycle) to replenish their thirst for San Miguel beer, inviting the driver to come in, and Eicher would buy him a beer. Six beers apiece later, they were off to Subic City's fantasy land determined to find Rod Stewart's "Shanghai Lil" (1971), whether she used the pill or not. Unbeknownst to Eicher and Vanzetti, the driver couldn't hold his beer and passed out. Vanzetti got behind the wheel and carried on. Eicher and the driver were down for the count, passed out on the floor, rolling back and forth in tandem as the jeepney had trouble remaining on the road. Vanzetti hadn't been told about mixing beer and Mojo, not a pretty sight. Before reaching Subic City, the jeepney smacked into a ditch and there it stayed. Vanzetti recovered quickly, barfed, then pulled Eicher out of the back, the driver still comatose.

"Forget Subic City, Eicher, when that driver comes to, he'll blame us for his jeep in the ditch. We gotta head back to base."

Eicher was in no condition to put up an argument. Vanzetti led Eicher away from the scene and both caught a ride from a trike driver passing by. By the time they reached Olongapo, curfew had been called and the streets were deserted except for Philippine Constabulary. The two hid in an alley, a block away from the base gate, both at a loss as to their next move. "If we could get past those PC at the gate, the marines would surely let us in," Vanzetti plotted. "Let's wait a few, maybe the PC will leave." Half an hour later, the original jeepney driver showed up screaming to the PC that two American sailors had wrecked his jeep. He conveniently left out why they had to drive it.

"That's it, we're busted," Eicher managed to say after barfing in someone's flowerpot.

"Follow me."

The two drunk shadows-in-the-night managed to find an area, shielded from the guards, where they descended to the banks of the river. The base fence lay beyond. "All we have to do is cross the river and climb the fence," Vanzetti said turning to Eicher.

"Ugh…that god-awful smell would gag a maggot," Eicher moaned.

"The water, can you swim?"

"Yes, in water…not across that. Didn't you see those kids under the bridge when we crossed? They beg sailors to throw a peso into the river so they can dive in to retrieve it. Any hair left on their head is orange."

Vanzetti got in Eicher's face with desperation. "We won't be diving to the bottom, Eicher. Just dog-paddle the fuck across. Try not to gargle. Can you make it, don't look more than fifty feet?"

"If I go under, you coming after me?"

"Hell no! You go under in that muck, your good as dead. You wouldn't want me to die too?"

"You wouldn't like my answer," Eicher said, still gagging at the horrendous smell.

They slowly entered the river, working their hands and arms keeping their heads above the muck. The opposite bank seemed as far away as the golden shores of California. After reaching the base side, the two climbed the bank, looked at each other, and promptly upchucked. Sewage-type slime began from the top of their neck down. Bloodshot and bulging out of their sockets, Eicher's eyes said it all. "My skin is burning like fire," he moaned in agony.

"Don't think about anything but getting over that fence," Vanzetti grimaced.

They made it to the motor pool, hosed off, and went to the barracks. Two days later at work, Vanzetti seemed concerned enough to pull me aside in confidence. "You did what?" Completely flabbergasted at these two Abbott-and-Costello-caliber idiots, I held my tongue out of admiration for their tenacity outmaneuvering the PC—but at what cost? "You'll have to decide, go to medical for a complete checkup. Who knows what swam up your bunghole, even your crank? They'll file a report and command will find out. You'll be on a plane to the states in hours. Or keep your lip zipped. Tough it out, hoping your kids don't come out looking like a jungle version of Ferdinand Marcos. Hell, half of Olongapo's sewage is drained out that river into the bay when the tide flushes its banks." Hearing that, Vanzetti's eyes transformed from a twenty-year-old to those of an eighty.

They stood fast. "Struggle through barbed-wire, suffer hell-fire from above, I'll even outrun the hound dogs…babe, just to have your love," Bob Dylan (1975). This duty was too exceptional to waste on healthcare at twenty years old.

Shore Patrol had their hands full every night. When multiple ships were anchored, more people were on liberty. Sailors + marines + alcohol = mayhem; overcrowded dancefloors; streets of chaos with thieves and opportunists making an easy roll of a stumbling drunk into an alley; no-excuse open brawling; like a moth to a flame, I found it all thrillingly magnetic. Sunrise brought as close to an antiseptic bath over, what a few hours before, was full of humanity in all its forms, to now—desolation row. Preparation for the next night's adventure, beginning anew. Totally intoxicating; this localized navy-marine-Filipino version was every bit the same as Bourbon Street during Mardi Gras. This bloody-knuckle and black-eye circus repeated itself every time the fleet was in harbor; wouldn't miss it. I did skip out the night my son was born.

Remaining successfully married within the socialized environment Olongapo presented was obviously more difficult for some than others; take for example the dastardly case of Rod, also as myself, married to a Filipina. Some sailors went to extra effort revolving around Subic Bay from one tour of duty to the next, be it extending, reenlisting, or cross-decking from one ship to another. Quite a paper-shuffling process, all to stay attached to a local honey or honeys. An air traffic controller whose sarcastic viewpoints kept me entertained, Rod had transferred in months back from the carrier Midway, joining his family already living in Olongapo.

UA from duty, we began a search for Rod. No answer at home, I located the sailor on the table in sickbay, up the hill at medical. Patched up from black-eyes and contusions around a swollen face, I arrived to ask what I could do for him in this condition, maybe locate and advise his wife. Cold fear replaced the normal sarcasm, his enlarged eyelids took on the look of a couple ripe purple plums ready to pop. He began begging me to keep his wife away from him, wanting to know if she was anywhere close by. I told him I'd help in any way possible, but he had to give up the story behind his condition. Absent any alternative, Rod 'fessed up saying his wife put him there.

"How could she do this, what'd you do, Rod?"

"After the day watch yesterday, Higgins and I rode our cycles out to Subic City."

Subic City was a hamlet where a group of brothels and nightclubs existed for sailors who needed what they came for in a hurry—no time for buying drinks and that foo-foo stuff.

"I can understand Higgins making that drive, Rod."

"Well…I wanted to show him the way. His first time and all, but I started drinking." Hours later from the bed of some woman he'd never known, Rod's conscience caught up with his deeds. He set about returning to his wife immediately. Entering his dark bedroom polluted as ever, Rod slipped into his bed next to his rightfully inquisitive wife. Last thing Rod, in his condition, was up for was that pesky need of communication in a marriage. Foregoing such trivialities in his view, Rod rolled over and planted a very wet, sloppy kiss on his wife's lips. Bedside lamp flared, his wife rolled out of bed toward the bathroom sink where, in the mirror, she observed blood around her mouth with a disgusting taste associated with said blood. Rod lost consciousness soon thereafter, ending up on the gurney where he now lay. I promised "Red-Wings Rod" I'd never divulge the details to the office which until now has been the case. Who knew, perhaps his wife was the forgiving kind? "Dream On" Aerosmith (1975).

Subic Bay Ship Repair Facility; Cubi Point Naval Air Station; on-base housing and off-base civilian city of Olongapo; all were surrounded on three sides by jungle. The military hospital sat farther up the hill past three miles of jungle terrain that one could expect the next *King Kong* movie to be filmed. Gangs of monkeys were prevalent. Insects and small animals—some we're used to in the US—have doubled, some even tripled in size as if this tropical climate was manipulated by a Dr. Boris Karloff.

Sita's awaiting her prenatal exam inside; I'm relaxed outside on the bike observing monkeys. The larger dominant male had just escorted one of his female concubines toward hump city no more than twenty-five yards away near the jungle's edge when he turned, looked at me, and stopped; his one objective throughout his day is keeping rival males from his harem. Catching me watching them obviously became an impediment against him and said concubine, completing the distance to hump city. The timing of his charge through dense undergrowth directly toward me, left in question the hustle factor one doesn't usually practice but only encounters rarely in extreme situations. Prior to realizing his intentions as the distance between us lessened by half, the surprisingly long teeth this four-foot male monkey garnished, spurred enough adrenaline to crank the bike, roll the throttle, and pray. Teeth eerily familiar from a Yosemite bear's charge last year.

Just down the hall the night my son was born, the hospital emergency room was bustling. Despite everything happening, I did know two carriers were in port plus the smaller escort ships; we're talking an easy fifteen thousand people on liberty. My infant son, not more than forty-five minutes, old, lay on the other side of a glass as I stood in amazement. A sailor, just bandaged from a stab wound to his shoulder during a bar fight, asked what ship I was from. "I'm 'station-dito'," I replied, a Tagalog term used by locals describing a sailor stationed here. From his face, he was in obvious pain or confusion from my answer, and I followed up saying that I was here for two years.

"How did you get those orders"? he cried, turning away.

"Just lucky." Could it have been more obvious? The heightened anxiety of thousands of young men, couped up in ships at sea for months, needed the release Olongapo provided. These walking, talking vials of testosterone, able to release pent-up stress with free-flowing alcohol at the hand of willing females, wouldn't allow mere stab wounds to cloud their liberty in the PI. "Damn the social diseases, unlock the hatches, we're on the loose again!"

Staring into the kelp beds of the Pacific off Monterey Bay back in California last year, I knew it must be more beautiful under the water. Scuba lessons I'd signed up for in Lemoore began without me due to a horrendous cold I'd caught. Bad luck I presumed; walking out of viewing the movie *Jaws* two weeks later, I knew it was a stroke of fate. Now in this tropical paradise, the timidity waned. Yes, sharks were in the area. Confronted daily with world-class conditions for snorkeling in these bluest of waters, I knew it couldn't be passed up. As if in a well-manicured fish tank, the unexpected colors were vividly spectacular—beautiful saltwater fish matched only by different shades of coral.

AC1 Ellinder completed the daily Notice to Airman brief before we assumed the oncoming eight-hour watch. Ed walked by, capturing Ellinder's attention. If there was a hybrid between Bigfoot and humans, Ed was it for no other reason than being hairy. His ears, forehead, and upper cheeks lacked hair, not so elsewhere. Some Italian mother somewhere was surely proud of her hairy son. Ed caught the crabs after spending the night out last month. Within two days, Ed walked into the social hygiene clinic looking as if he'd come in from a blizzard. The female hospital corpsman at the dispensary called the next patient in order as per the check-in log. Ed, along with sailors and marines, waited their turn; hacking coughs abundant, a sailor on crutches, a grunt, squirming in his seat, trying to hold a full bladder for an upcoming urine specimen, a dozen in all. Despite the crutches, an arriving sailor joined all others on one side of the waiting room away from Ed. The corpsman, noticing the situation, approached Ed then stopped three feet away. Initially, Ed appeared older with gray hair. She couldn't quite focus until she grabbed her reading glasses hanging around her neck. Vision now focused, the corpsman's initial thought was of a snow globe she had as a child. As realization smacked her cheek, she retreated to the others and promptly lost it. According to Ed, "She made the others evacuate and left me in the room. Five minutes later, she returns with something like a hazmat suit on." Ed was a hairball.

Post muster, Ellinder begins telling Ed about an uninhabited Capones Island, about thirty miles up the coast, well known for its unmatched, underwater beauty. The next Friday before sunrise, the three of us headed north up the coast. I hired a *banka* boat driver to deliver us to the island for 100 pesos with his promise to return at 1600 for a 150-peso pickup. Mask, snorkel, fins, and ice chest of beer; we were set. Each of us split up picking a stretch of beach to prowl. Absolute beach heaven! I snorkeled to no farther than a 25 ft. depth from which I could dive among colorful specimens of coral. Half-hour later, I added a nice-sized lobster to our ice chest, now low on beer. The deserted beach left me ready to return to the surf.

Fifty yards offshore, I dove into the world's largest aquarium. Around twenty feet into my dive, movement to my left caught my attention when the profile of an approaching shark filled my mask. Having deliberated for months the odds of confronting a shark, I'd convinced myself scenes from *Jaws* were just that, a movie. Excerpts from those moments as a kid at the Delta Theatre seeing a closeup of *Creature from the Black Lagoon* (1954) or giant ants from *Them* (1954) tearing through human bodies—scenes which had created what I thought was maximum fear paled in comparison. A fountain of unknown origin exploded, what I surely hoped was, enough adrenaline to boost my initial stage of retreat.

Fins, attached to my kicking legs, thankfully propelled me, as quick as humanly possible but parallel to the beach. Visions of underwater scenes, Peter Benchley could have certainly used in his movie consuming my thoughts, I refused to waste a millisecond glancing backward. Crossing a trench in the seabed, my body began tumbling out of control. Caught in some invisible underwater current, I fought to gain some buoyancy—at least know up from down. Grabbing for any handhold, my body encountered razor-sharp edges of coral and rock formations slicing and dicing every surface it encountered. After forty-five seconds of this, my lungs were void of all air, but my feet touched sand as my head broke the water's surface, teeth from a shark's open mouth, heading my way occupied 99.9 percent of all conscious thought.

Surf lapped over my prone body mere feet from the beach. Farther underwater exploration was immediately relegated to the Jacques Cousteaus of the world. Blood oozed from tiny cuts all over my body—a homing beacon for all sharks within miles. Tim McCracken, a friend found dead in the surf off Jax beach three years before, took my arm and walked me back up the surf. God-awful thirsty, only lobster eyes from the cooler, seemingly with delight at my plight, compared my dire state to its own then one-upped me. "Beers gone...damn those guys!"

Mc and I may as well have been on Jax Beach just before he walked away; his exact voice from half a world away explaining my good luck versus his bad when the underwater current had shanghaied my retreat. "The speeding underwater current in the ocean-floor trough was cycling toward the beach instead of back out to sea, right into the shark's waiting mouth," Mc informed me.

Can't explain it, nor do I have to. In my condition, an old friend helped soothe my need. "Bridge of Sighs" Robin Trower (1974). Thirsty with two hours till pickup, I lay in the shade of a coconut tree, looked up, smiled, and grabbed my knife. That night, I ate the best damn lobster of my life next to a place-setting always available for Tim McCracken.

Time for reenlistment. Local scuttlebutt had guys, in my situation, simply getting on a jet for home leaving "supposed loved ones" behind. Wasn't within me to do such. My decision had been made before I'd married. Bargaining on the phone with navy detailers, at the Pentagon in Washington DC, seemed easy if your work evaluations proved your worth. I held back for orders to the closest naval air station to my hometown. They delivered: Belle Chasse, Louisiana.

Walking past Cubi Point base operations before leaving the building, this female controller was at her desk sobbing. Quite unusual at work, I instantly thought of Regina back in Lemoore, when her husband died. Asked if she needed anything, "Elvis just died," was her reply. Okay, my hands were tied on that one.

Three cases of San Miguel beer and two pitchers of Mojo (a concoction guaranteed to "light the fires and kick the tires" at any gathering) provided the needed elixir to get the skids greased for a dozen or so well-wishers. Neighbors on both sides of my housing unit were also invited, of course, to expand the party perimeter. These new housing units carved out of the surrounding jungle by Seabees had just been completed. We had been living up here in the hills above Subic Bay for four months; jungle-critters displaced by the construction, continued showing up in all manners; rats the size of opossums digging through dumpsters and pythons stopping traffic, while crossing the road.

Tracker, an acquaintance from back in Lemoore, showed up since the carrier he was now on was in port. "Harper, you move by leaps and bounds. Year and a half ago, a single dude, today, married and dad of three.

"How's the family?" I asked.

"Separated. She's living with her parents."

"I've got just the medicine you need, meet Dr. Mojo."

Robin Trower's guitar rowed a slow pirogue through the soupiest blues this side of a Louisiana swamp. The first pitcher of Mojo had disappeared. Over the sound of the music and general mayhem came a blood curdling scream echoing in and outside. People, from drunk to sober, stopped. I ran out the back sliding glass door into the yard—nothing. Another scream, as thirty seconds before, but shorter this time coming from next door. My neighbor found a five-foot cobra on her bedroom floor. Yes! Fang city, ready to dispense their deadly poison—not quite as potent as Mojo but enough to call security. Two animal control officers, with a security escort, responded, capturing the displaced snake which had slithered in through a sliding door left open by inches.

Before leaving, security stopped by saying a big investigation was going on in Olongapo that night. Two navy chief petty officers were having a retirement ceremony at a club when butterfly knives began flying. Both had been murdered.

Naval Investigative Service, Philippine Embassy in Manila, US Embassy in Manila—all wanted a piece of us. Three-hour trips to Manila became common, each office requiring documents. A Vesuvius of paperwork erupted, which when filed, required "greasing" each receiving palm with pesos, if I was to walk away hoping the filed paperwork moved up the chain. Adamant corruption top to bottom. Some sense of entitlement was owed Filipinos by Americans, had to be. Any public official with an opportunity to shake down someone for cash, they took it. Each clerk knew they had us over a barrel because of time constraints. I paid up; surely the origin of a hiatal hernia occurring later. Paperwork, visas, passports all in hand, we boarded the aircraft in October of '77, sweating bullets; some official would pull us aside because of some undotted i requiring one thousand pesos to correct.

NAS New Orleans, Louisiana— January 1978

Crescent City Connection spanned the Mississippi River from east to west bank. Seven miles, as the pelican flies south of GNO, sits the naval air station in Belle Chasse just within Plaquemines Parish. Surrounded by low-lying swamp, bayous, the Intercoastal Canal, and the Mississippi River, the airport essentially floats on centuries worth of river-delta bogs, ripe with swamp critters, especially alligator and moccasin.

I felt as if I'd come full circle, returning to my home state. Stateside employment had been a prerequisite to bring home immigrants. The deal back overseas, promised the French Quarter, and here it was. Not a stranger to the city, I'd visited numerous times growing up. Stacked against other US cities, New Orleans pretty much reigns over others with entertainment and cuisine. People here loved to get very merry; habits similar to sailors and marines on liberty back in Subic Bay. The French Quarter, however, had just as many alleyways as Magsaysay—ones also leading down a one-way rabbit hole.

In 1978, a family of five living for seven months in a small apartment on E-5 wages made an opening in on-base housing seem like a pay raise. Finally in-base housing without a monthly electric bill in New Orleans frees up a little cash, enough to drive a '79 Plymouth Volare station wagon owned by the Navy Federal Credit Union. The old '64 Pontiac Catalina from Oakdale had been used to scour out the bottom of potholes around New Orleans as well as teach the wife to drive. Work schedules were arranged; wife working now, allowed her or myself at home with the three children ages four, two, and one. *Yes*, work intensity at home trumped air traffic control.

SCUTTLEBUTT

The two prior airports I'd worked gave me no opportunity to utilize the other half of ATC's function, radar. New Orleans offered that opportunity. The air traffic didn't have the firebrand intensity as Lemoore or Cubi Point, but both radar and tower were needed for rate advancement. Operating radar was a totally different animal; challenging and magnetic to the appeal. Facility watch supervisor guaranteed less time off; however no more training.

2115 local time, Louisiana Air National Guard squadron of A-37s and VP-94's unit of P-3s were finishing up their daily schedule with Air Force Reserve's F-100 fighter squadron already secured earlier. A C-130 Hurricane Hunter out of Biloxi had been in the GCA radar pattern for a half hour. Occasional transient aircraft, as in the A-4 Skyhawk Attack jet also under radar control on final approach at three miles, were inbound. I pushed the clearance to land button on the tower's console, indicating to the radar controller down in the radar room that he could issue the Skyhawk its clearance to land.

The A-4 had been the type of jet the most honorable navy pilot I could remember; John McCain had been flying over North Vietnam when anti-aircraft fire shot the Skyhawk down. As you probably know, somehow surviving the ejection with two broken arms in the water of a rice paddy, McCain endured beating by his captors only to be sent to the Hanoi Hilton for years of torture and the heroic epic in which he conducted himself therein.

This Skyhawk exited the runway for overnight parking and a refuel. Transient line called the tower, once the aircraft was chocked, wanting to know what was on the A-4s fuel probe. I couldn't leave the tower, so I instructed the caller to position his pickup's headlights on the probe so I could view with my long eyes. Smack dab through the center of a round disk was the business end of the probe. The A-4s external probe is parallel to the cockpit and even with the nosecone. It reminded me of the round centerline reflector located on a pole a few feet above the ground just short of the runway threshold. I requested the support person drive to the reflectors location which he then advised was missing. What the hell?

I requested the fire chief on duty check the A-4 for any damages, which there were none. I called the tower chief, AC1 Striker, who advised me to mark the recording tapes for analyzation tomorrow. Somehow the Skyhawk had dipped below glideslope angle on short final, impaling a centerline reflector with a bull's-eye undeterred. Merrily on its way, the jet continued another five seconds, reaching the runway threshold with a normal rollout. How was the pilot not aware? Worse yet, how was the tower controller not aware? Uh-oh... "Tubular Bells" (1973), theme song from *The Exorcist*, began at low volume, tickling my inner ear.

Gene had been my mentor from my check in, and as my section leader, we'd worked extensively together. He asked if was I distracted. As I began to respond with "Of course not," it clicked in my mind. Somewhere in that timespan, the ground controller had ask to switch the weather vision monitor to a local television station, which was *taboo*—not allowed. Hating to then admit what I'd just remembered, I couldn't lie to Gene. We wrote up the report, knowing I was biting the bullet on this one. "In this business, the supervisor must be a stickler for the little rules, seemingly unimportant at the moment, yet were written down in the past from the blood of those who've flown before," Gene stressed. The next day, expecting to finish out my enlistment parking transient aircraft, I reported to the tower chief. Gene said he'd talk to the brass. They agreed my experience was needed, and this was to be my one and only mistake. People come and go in our lives; a select few, with their strength of character, stand in your defense if they have reason to believe in you. Striker deserves his well-placed position in my hall of memories.

The Cars, Neil Young, and AC/DC were vibrating the airwaves with needed relief. The ever-present need for sharp awareness at both work and home with the kids, made escape, when possible, extremely valuable. Thrills normally associated with New Orleans didn't cater to young children but remembering the joy a simple picnic could bring did. On the Algiers levee of the Mississippi River; under a mammoth live oak tree in Audubon Park; roller coaster at Pontchartrain Beach; anywhere safe fun could be had, we went. When extra coins were available, *Star Wars* movies or the latest Clint Eastwood shoot-'em-up couldn't be missed. The kids were introduced to the more PG Mardi Gras parades held on the west bank. Plastic beads and doubloons were a thrill at least until they got home. I mentioned safe specifically for the reason our children were accident prone. One might suggest parents are responsible for a safe environment; agreed, however, seconds are all it takes for disaster. My youngest son jumping off the top rung of a slide's ladder while yelling, "Superman!"; my other son jumping from the air conditioner next to our housing unit; my daughter hanging upside down from a monkey bar at my sister's home in Oakdale; all within six months and each with a broken arm.

Doug stood in the center of the tower, headset cord stretching to reach his position. I was plugged into Ground Control combined with Flight Data and Tower Supervisor.

"Jazz 21 and flight, Navy New Orleans Tower, report the initial runway 22, wind 210 at 14, altimeter 30.01, traffic C-130 five miles east of the airport at 2000 feet."

Jazz 21 advised, "Roger."

Doug called down to radar, "GCA, Tower. Traffic flight of two F-15s approaching initial, DB."

"Tower, GCA. Roger, DH."

A thunderous boom erupted, shaking windows. We both look around to see billowing smoke and fire erupting from an oil rig under construction in the Mississippi River, just off base approximately one and a half miles away from the tower.

"Navy Tower, Jazz 21 initial, just observed an explosion on the oil rig in the Mississippi River east of your location."

"Jazz 21 over the numbers right break approved, copy your report, we're aware."

"Roger."

From the tower we see, what is now, a hundred-foot ball of flames over the oil rig's position. Although close to the base and airport operations, the navy has no jurisdiction over the scene. Alerting control facilities of the situation, I also get on the phone to the ATC office advising them. Doug clears the flight of F-15s to land.

"Navy New Orleans Tower, CG1801 for departure to assist in the oil rig fire."

"CG1801, wind 200 at 8, cleared for takeoff."

The operations officer rang the buzzer at the tower door for entrance. Seeing the unfolding scene from the tower's level, he turned and said, "Suspend all outbound flights until advised, inbounds restricted to full stop only. There'll be news choppers swarming within ten minutes. Do your job but give leeway to those news guys, we don't need any bad press." We passed the word to radar and Moisant Approach. Flames were lower but black smoke obstructed a good half of the airport traffic area. I told radar and approach the local pattern was closed, straight ins only to a full stop.

Until fireboats from New Orleans could make it down the river to the scene, minimum assistance from the rig crew itself would have to suffice in any rescue operations along with local Belle Chasse fire-fighting units and the coast guard helo launched earlier. Base crash fire sent a couple trucks just off base to the scene but radioed back that they couldn't reach the area around the moored rig. A second explosion, from a compressed gas tank attached to the rig, added to the mayhem surrounding the site. Multiple municipal rescue helicopters checked-in enroute to the area.

"Doug, you're about to get bombarded with helos out the ying-yang, how are you going to handle it?" As tower supervisor I needed to know.

"Have them maintain visual separation from one another."

"As well as?" I stressed. "Advise each one checking in of the smoke obstruction. Keep a list of callsigns and type so you'll know how many choppers are within our area, which means, they must call you departing the area. Keep your approach corridor clear. Have helos in that area circumnavigate to the rig. If you need help, put it on speaker and I'll lend a hand."

For two hours, airport operations were restricted while the rig construction's safety procedures were put to the test. Rapid-response helos from the city and the base helped where necessary, while national news coverage jumped into the fray. All said and done, three construction workers went to the hospital and a lot of investment up in smoke.

The most positive advantage to working in New Orleans was leaving it for Oakdale; less than four hours north. The contrast between the two could not have been more. I wanted the children to know my family. Dad also needed occasional help that I could provide; win-win situation. On one fateful trip toward Oakdale, backseat lowered so the kids would nap, the '79 Plymouth Volare wagon was shy of Baton Rouge about fifteen miles when all hell broke loose. My grip on the wheel tightened upon hearing the thump, thump, sound, seemingly overhead as if a helicopter was directly above the car. In the left lane, having just passed a vehicle on the right, the steering wheel yanked from my grip, sending the car immediately into clockwise donuts. Wife screaming, kids' bodies bouncing around the car's interior like a ping-pong lottery drawing. Grabbing the wheel, I stopped the spinning, glaring through the windshield, expecting an onslaught of incoming traffic. Opposite direction traffic sailed past our wagon as we sat, miraculously, on the right shoulder facing oncoming Friday afternoon I-10 westbound traffic. A thicker coat of paint and traffic would have scrapped the passenger side of the car. Beyond shock, everyone seemed okay as I ordered, "Seatbelts on...now!"

Both rear tires were flat. With one spare on hand, I removed the tire on the side of the car, away from traffic, and scampered across the median with my family locked in the car. Eventually, a VW bug driver, my good Samaritan, had mercy on some stranger holding a flat tire in one arm. The closer town was just back down I-10, probably Sorento. Tire plugged and aired up, I was heading back to I-10 when thankfully a state cop gave assistance with a lift back, positioning his vehicle so I could replace both rear tires. Mandatory seatbelts were the new order.

October '79, summer heat enveloped all of bayou country from Lake Pontchartrain across the Atchafalaya Basin all the way to the Sabine Pass. "God awful humidity in New Orleans was surely sent from hell itself." Television ministers found any tongue-twisting way to blame the weather on hell-bound sinners known to populate the French Quarter. Wouldn't you know it, up brews a hurricane passing through the Lesser Antilles toward the Gulf of Mexico. Despite soothsayers egging on death and destruction, others lay back unconcerned. Hurricane Bob had New Orleans in its crosshairs. Two days and counting, landfall appears imminent. Navy command authorized "hurricane departures" of aircraft as the military base buttoned down. Family sent north early in the week, I remained with a contingent of others for the needs of the base.

Hurricane Bob made landfall in Terrebonne Bay, spawning enough super thunderstorms that tornados were rampant. Electronics in the tower had been affected, rendering it down temporarily. As weather improved, we cranked up the mobile MRC-131 communications truck and headed out toward the runway to communicate and control inbound, returning aircraft after a return-to-normal had begun. Low-lying ground was extremely saturated, we remained on hard surface. Much of the ramp surface was inundated however, draining back into the bayous and swamps.

Using a variety of communications gear, we set up and began operation on location. Ballard, a controller new to the New Orleans area, sat in the passenger seat. Moisant Approach Control called on my mobile-handheld advising of a flight of five F-100s, passing over De La Croix, were inbound for an overhead approach. Before setting up adjacent the runway, we had conducted a visual sweep of the landing surface finding it clear of debris and adequate for landing.

"Navy New Orleans Tower, Saint 69, flight of five, at the initial."

Through the portable radios of the vehicle, I broadcast, "Saint 69 runway 22, right traffic, altimeter 29.69, no reported traffic, break right over the numbers, report base." Ballard picked up the FM radio and called Nola Fire for a standby crash truck due to incoming traffic.

"Tower, Saint 69 and flight base leg for landing."

"Saint 69, Navy Tower, maintain pilot separation on rollout, check wheels down, wind 200 at 12, cleared to land." I responded as the crash truck took up position, approximately one hundred feet to our right. NOLA 6 rolled to a stop and called the tower.

"NOLA Tower, NOLA 6."

"Go ahead."

"You need to look to the ground out your vehicle's window."

Ballard and I look at one another, as if to confirm we'd heard him correctly, then looked out the window—not up but down. In front of the MRC-131 lay a twelve-foot alligator along with its ten-foot mate under the truck. Ballard started screaming.

Exiting the runway near our position, the flight leader keyed his microphone, "Navy Tower, Saint 69 clearing the runway, ah…you have a gator problem, boy."

"Roger, we're aware, taxi to your line."

"Say again, I hear screaming."

"We're fine. Taxi to your line."

The fire truck approached our vehicle slowly. "Ballard… shut up." From Utah, where a gator's pearly whites never sparkle, his screaming slowed while his anxiety pegged. The MRC-131 was blocked from moving unless I went rogue on the ten-footer lying under the truck. I asked the firetruck to maneuver his vehicle and ride herd on the twelve-footer.

They responded, "NOLA Tower, NOLA 6. This truck would sink to its axles in the wet sod."

At this delay, Ballard amped up the decibels. WTF! Short of Jedi mind-trickin' my cohort in the passenger seat, I cranked the MRC-131, slammed it in reverse, then popped the clutch. The front wheels hit the ten-foot gator and stopped. The gator's tail, surely in a retaliatory move, smacked the side of truck, breaking off a vital antenna for the radio. SOB! Surely, it would now move. It didn't. I revved the engine and changed gears. Ballard, not someone to take camping, began moaning. In first gear this time, the truck's rear wheels made it over the gator. Nasty critters! Enroute to the ET shop, Ballard said he needed a head break. Figured he'd probably be changing skivvies.

New Orleans took a toll on the relationship in our marriage. We were at an impasse, the future of little children, hanging in the balance. To prevent some unwanted knockdown or drag out, I terminated shore duty opting for a ship, giving us some space. Love isn't always on time, "Hold the Line," Toto (1978). We all headed over to Mayport, Florida.

CV-59 USS *Forrestal*—August 1981

It was time. Transferring to a ship after eight plus years in the biggest canoe club around, I knew I still had dues to pay at sea. Stacked right next to that fact that Tim McCracken was urging me on. I knew, stepping onto the CV-59's brow, Mc would be with me, finally serving on an aircraft carrier, not nuclear but one just the same. Air traffic control onboard ship was an exotic breed of the land-based equivalent—a sea-safari requiring meticulous maneuvers to get the job done.

While the family settled into base housing, I concentrated learning shipboard life on CV-59, the very ship John McCain served on. A few years before off the coast of Vietnam, an explosion and deadly fire on Forrestal's flight deck occurred killing hundreds. CV-59 was now commencing workups in the Caribbean Sea between Cuba and Puerto Rico in preparation for a six-month Indian Ocean cruise starting in June '82.

Earning petty officer first-class stripes back in New Orleans, I was now granted little perks and privileges to shipboard life. The navy is structured by a ranking system even more pronounced on a ship. Berthing compartments, ship corridors, storage areas, hangar bays, and workspaces all comprising a floating airport look amazingly the same once inside the ship. Others in the distant past, obviously struck with my current plight, decided labeling corridors, levels, and compartments with specific numbering would be beneficial for those like me. Getting my bearings took a solid week. Battle readiness required proving I could, while blindfolded, get from my rack to an outside access if the ship lost power, was under attack, maybe sinking—Titanic? Those old *Victory at Sea* reels now seemed much more relevant. This job had risks of life or death. Not knowing at that time seven Forrestal sailors would lose their lives on the upcoming cruise; we prepared each day with caution. This ship had a mission requirement—all else be damned!

All aircraft depend upon lift from approaching wind to depart as well as land. Aircraft carriers at sea use their mobility to turn into the new direction the wind is blowing from. Pete and I were the two designated radar final controllers, each operating a monstrosity of a console, every bit the size of a plush loveseat which wrapped around the controller. Dozens of internally lit indicator lights available if needed with a push of a finger, surrounded the radar scope in the center. Memphis Naval Training Center had trained us in its usage.

As flights returned post-mission, marshal control stacked them at different altitudes awaiting a push time when the ship was ready for recovery. At a certain prescribed time, individual aircraft checked into approach control, shuffling arrivals into back-to-back handoffs to Pete and me. We kept each aircraft aligned to the ship's final bearing and descending at a prescribed rate to ensure each aircraft is at the precise point on final approach for the landing signal officer. The arresting gear cable, used as each landing aircraft's tailhook snags it, was reset before the next aircraft crossed the ship's aft end, the round down. A bumper sticker I'd seen, "Air Traffic Controllers do it with minimum separation," surely evolved from such situations.

Typically, mission plans involved various type naval aircraft on board; be it electronic surveillance, tankers, attack, or fighter type; post mission, they land in sequence. Pete and I issued direction of flight, separation, and altitude assistance simultaneously to successive aircraft on their final approach. Navy aircraft were given a nine-to-ten-mile straight-in glidepath approach. Pete and I each, had separate radio frequencies controlling upward of three separate aircraft simultaneously, lined up on final to the ship. Frequency congestion had to be minimized. Excess chatter wasn't possible.

During aircraft recovery, the carrier always sails into the wind, turning, sometimes chasing, the wind's direction to aid the aircraft. The ship's new heading after a turn, altered the final bearing each aircraft on final had to receive; even more flight data to apply as intensity heightened.

Approximately a mile prior to the ship, each aircraft is handed off to the landing signal officer who visually prompts the aircraft toward the ship. Current pilots themselves, LSOs have about as dangerous of a job on the carrier as anyone. Less than a hundred feet from the ship's aft-end, on the port side, is the LSO platform adjacent to the Fresnel Lens. The corrugated metal walkway appears suspended over the ocean over a hundred feet below yet is attached with bolts only. I stood alongside these men on that platform, Mickey Mouse ears on for hearing protection, watching the ship's recovery of jet aircraft. Maybe fifty feet away from the center line the aircraft are aiming to land on, the LSO advises each aircraft of their relative position toward a safe landing. A pilot's error on short final could take out anyone or all the people on the LSO platform. It has happened more than once on different aircraft carriers, thankfully not when I visited.

One such aircraft, an F-4 phantom crossed the round down too low, striking the end of the ship. The jet broke in half, sending all on the LSO platform diving through an open hatch into the ship for cover. The aircraft's rear half fell into the ocean behind the ship, while its forward section with both pilots, began sliding across the flight deck angling toward the side of the ship. This deck is the roof of our control room where the sound of the scraping metal overhead, made our cringe-factor explode above everything else.

A closed-circuit television covering operations on the flight deck, provided visual images of the scene real time, for us one deck below. I broke off approaches for aircraft under my control, issuing a foul deck call. The phantom's lead pilot popped the canopy and ejected; the second remained. "*Eject! Eject!*" Everyone observing the closed-circuit TV yelled. We watched, along with the husband and father of a newborn, the backseat navy lieutenant's last seconds of life on earth. Unconscious or unable, he remained in the backseat unmoved, possibly watching, front half of the phantom sliding, metal on metal, over the edge disappearing into the depths. As busy as controllers were at that moment, marshal controller, approach, and final, seeing this we stopped; dead silence for five seconds. Lead pilot with parachute closely behind landed safely on the flight deck.

Fighting the bitter taste associated with death, a retched bile I've come to expect from the growing amount witnessed, I and the other controllers reestablished radar contact. With multiple airborne aircraft waiting their turn at the flying fuel pumps tanker A-6 jets, senior chief in CATTC (Carrier Air Traffic Control Center) issued orders to rendezvous all available fuel tankers with remaining aircraft having a low-fuel state. Planned out, the arrival of remaining aircraft aloft would commence when the "air boss" gave the signal. Search and rescue helicopter performed the task of looking for the missing pilot. Not surprisingly, he was lost at sea.

This F-4 squadron's bad luck hadn't just started with this event. Within the northern portion of, yes, the Bermuda Triangle, the Forrestal's Atlantic eastbound transit had been in full steam. Approaching noon on a beautiful sunny morning with full-blown flight operations yet to commence, the CO of this fighter squadron and his backseat pilot were poised on the flight deck for a single-aircraft mission. The F-4's nose-gear was attached to the bridle hook of the Forrestal's hydraulic system. To compensate for lacking a full-length runway, this system gave departing aircraft a boost. This, combined with the aircraft's self-generated power, achieved enough lift into the wind, to get airborne off the length of the carrier. They were given the okay by the air boss for departure.

Onto vulture's row, an elevated observation platform on the carrier's island, Tony and I stepped through the water-tight door armed with Wayfarer sunglasses, earplugs, blankets, and sunscreen. The time to catch a few rays came little, as of late. Tony, one of the approach controllers, asked, "Did you know the mess cranks will cook up your own surf-and-turf birthday meal, as in steak and lobster tail, down in the mess hall? Just show up and prove your birthday with your ID, that simple."

"Had no idea. Two and a half months countdown begins now." I said as a spurt of sun lotion shot into my palm and a loud thud accompanied an F-4's launch. We looked over the four-foot wall down below to see the phantom jet floundering just ahead of the ship. The ship's hydraulic system had malfunctioned during the F-4's launch.

In full view of all watching, the aircraft struggled without enough air flow and speed for that essential lift then dropped. No more than a mile ahead of the ship, both pilots ejected just prior to the aircraft's splashdown. The ship commenced an immediate starboard turn to prevent overrunning the pilots now in the water. Tony and I were standing on the elevated island taking it all in, as if we were behind the wheel of the ship maneuvering the beast hoping to not overrun two of the navy's best, just ahead. We had a visual of the parachutes and shroud lines atop the surface. The SAR helo approached. The carrier's length, amidst the starboard turn, was the immediate factor we knew was critical. No matter how promptly the helo got into position to conduct the rescue, the rapidly approaching aft of the ship appeared to make the whole evolution for naught. Turning this size of a ship, having been underway at around twenty-five knots, within that short distance is a herculean feat. The ships fantail cleared the incident sight by approximately fifty yards. For an aircraft carrier at sea that distance is as miniscule as the fuzz on a peach's bottom.

I noticed one of the floating parachutes had disappeared as search and rescue jumpers plunged into the sea. The F-4, now joining previous victimized ships and planes throughout the Bermuda Triangle, took its place in Davy Jones' Locker. The backseat pilot, entangled in his parachute's cords, had sank along with the phantom. We watched the other rescued pilot; the squadron's CO, now within the helo's rescue hoist, retract upward to safety. This was the same pilot which, later in the cruise, would survive another ejection onto the carrier's flightdeck in the incident described prior to this. Obviously, experience pays off. Whatever amount these pilots with balls of steel are paid, it just couldn't be enough.

The only space for privacy was in my third rack-high bunk space enclosed in curtains. Retreat from these tombstone blues occurring with frequency was necessary. My portable listening device with headset played cassettes I'd recorded before leaving Mayport behind. As if on a "Crazy Train" (1981) sometimes, I understood Ozzy Osborne's decision to leave Black Sabbath; during CV-59's workup off the coast of Panama, "Running with the Devil" (1978) by Van Halen ripping the guitar strings; and Flock of Seagulls' "I Ran" (1982) among some of note.

As big as an aircraft carrier is, size matters—the immensity of the Indian Ocean that is. I stood on the flight deck observing sunrise, and a small, thirty-foot sailboat a mile off the starboard side. Regardless of who observed it first—those on the sailboat or me—contrast between an aircraft carrier and a single-mast sloop didn't matter, both so miniscule in such a vast body of water we could only hope for calm winds and following seas.

Having cancelled a port visit in Mozambique, off the east coast of Africa, due to Somalian terrorist being too much of a threat during liberty, we languished in the Indian Ocean for eighty-four days. Needing relief from constant operations, we headed back for the Suez Canal. During the canal's transit there would be no flight operations. A flight deck picnic was going down. Sailors brought up blankets, sunglasses, personal listening devices, and suntan lotion. Africa just below port side of the carrier with Saudi Arabia in the distance on the starboard. Majority of the 4,500 on board rarely had access to the sun. The crew's morale improved when it did.

Some sailors were at that point in their enlistment status where they had to decide to get out of the navy and go home or reenlist, continuing to sail the seven seas. Some of those deciding to remain chose the ship's Suez Canal transit for their reenlistment ceremony on the flight deck amid the sunbathers, as myself.

Quarter of a tube of Banana Boat later, I'm as greased as a pig on a spit. From the endless sand dunes of Saudi Arabia, I walked across the flight deck and look down upon more of the same in Africa. At least there are clusters of palm trees resembling the oasis we've seen in countless desert movies. No more than fifty yards away, I observe through my binoculars camels enjoying the extremely rare shade; tails wagging, constantly combating the dark cloud of flies swarming at their rearend. Hazards of any environment are to be expected wherever one goes. Back home, the swamps of Louisiana brought all sorts of hazards starting with mosquitos; here that pesky critter is the common blowfly.

I know the yada, yada, yada associated with each Joe Schmo's reenlistment ceremony—seven sailors total, now happening near mid ship. "Sympathy for the Devil" (1968) by the Rolling Stones is playing in my ear. Adjacent to the seven re-enlistees, all decked out in their tropical white uniform, are two tables. One for all the forms involved, the other to hold a monster-size sheet cake covered in wax paper until this very moment. Now, all these sailors on that flight deck could give a flying rat's ass about these guy's decision to reenlist. *Hello*…it's the cake. We all knew from experience when the cake-eating portion began; obvious as the crowd lined up for a sweet sliver of what at sea had become precious: white, buttercream frosted, sheet-cake. The surrounding crowd of, by now, drooling sailors, began lining up. Admittedly a sweet freak, I was one. It was then I noticed one of the re-enlistees, in tropical white uniform, was Hinson from my division who'd just made petty officer third class as well as now signing up for another enlistment. Within five seconds, the table-sized sheet cake changed from white to a "crawling black." Yeah, in my mind, I knew exactly where those pesky critters had flown directly from. Re-enlistees, the officer-in-charge, and those as myself now seemingly cursed with a sweet tooth, looked on in disgust at what could have been a righteous sugar fix.

Within two days, we're back to flight operations within the Mediterranean Sea. Night operations in full swing—the crew in CATCC have a recovery in progress. PO3 Hinson behind the lighted, plexiglass, status board, stood writing with a grease pencil the fuel state of the A-6 tankers. This flight cycle nearing completion, I have two aircraft on final approach. As I hand the last aircraft in the recovery over to the landing signal officer (LSO), the ship's claxon horn begins its loud warning, and the voice following warns all to "Man your battle stations." We were used to this in the form of the occasional drills the ship practices for the real thing. Was this the real thing?

Different spaces on the ship are divided up among the many divisions of personnel to be maintained. When the ship is at "battle stations," hatches leading to those spaces must be secured to create a water-tight integrity the ship must maintain at this elevated security risk. Already at our assigned place, CATCC, we still needed personnel to secure the assigned spaces. PO Hinson, coming out from behind the status boards, was directed by Senior Chief to head up to the island's radar dome to ensure hatches were secure. Assigned this duty before, he knew it involved climbing an external ladder to get to the space.

Within fifteen minutes, the operation's officer walks into our control room saying we were under battle stations because a Russian submarine had surfaced, crossing perpendicularly for a moment, in front of the ship's heading. These maneuvers weren't common but did occasionally happen. The Russian navy pulled tricks such as this to let us know they were monitoring us. The Forrestal's immediate response, rightfully so, was to prepare for battle if it needed to respond.

PO3 Hinson returned, visibly stunned—slack-jawed, if not completely goggle-eyed. Grabbing the first seat available as if his energy was spent, he appeared more confused than tired. Senior Chief approached, got Hinson some water, and waited. A couple minutes later, Hinson recounted, heading up to secure the hatch underneath the radar site. "Halfway up the ladder, I noticed the blanket of stars overhead...so bright. No sign of the moon. Reached the top, secured the hatch, and started down. It was off the starboard side of the fantail."

"What, Hinson, what the hell is this *it*?" Senior Chief demanded.

"I don't know, Senior. I just don't know. At first there was a bright light of some sort, under the surface. I stopped midway, down the ladder, watching it. The light broke the surface and shot up into the sky like a rocket until it was out of sight...without a sound."

Senior Chief sat back in his chair, eyes drilled into Hinson. "Now is not to the time for this bullshit!" The operations officer, hearing the account, told Senior Chief and Hinson to come with him as they left CATCC. All within earshot, me included, were dumbfounded. I turned to Pete, sitting next to me, "Hinson's is not a bullshitter...typically point on, he saw something."

The one MC announced, "Secure from battle stations." Immediately, Pete and I left in the direction of Hinson and his interrogators. Through operations, we headed toward the op officer's office. Normally open, the door was closed. I slowed, listened, and heard Hinson being questioned. Couldn't just stand there, so we kept going.

Now speculation set in. Russian sub, battle stations, a friggin' UFO—were they connected? Had that submarine crossed in front of our ship chasing who knows what? We had only questions. Pete and I headed down to berthing, deciding to wait there for Hinson. He never showed up. I went to my rack and tried to sleep but couldn't. Next morning at the breakfast table, the third cup of caffeine has my eyelids at attention when Pete's bloodshot eyes sit across and cry out, "Hinson's gone, rack's cleared out."

"No fucking way!"

In Senior Chief's office, we asked in unison, "Where's Hinson, Senior?"

Senior looked as if he'd last slept two weeks ago. "Hinson departed on the COD (carrier supply aircraft) this morning, he's on medical leave."

"I can't believe this, it's what he saw, isn't it?" I argued.

"Harper, calm down, Ops O. believes he needs some R & R, that's all."

"Right…guy did what he was supposed to do. Tells his senior what he sees, gets shitcanned! For God's sake, he just reenlisted," I posed.

"You two saddle up, we commence operations in fifteen." Senior Chief stopped all discussions.

Pete and I found out Hinson wasn't the only Forrestal sailor needing some so-called R & R. Three sailors total departed the ship while at sea that morning. Had they suddenly needed R & R after seeing what Hinson observed? We were left with only questions and speculation. Lesson learned by those in CATCC that night—anyone witnessing a mermaid off the brow getting humped by some alien, keep it to yourself.

Within the Mediterranean Sea again, we made up for lost time with three port visits in the three remaining months of the cruise. The Forrestal dropped anchor in Alexandria, Egypt, only to be told no eating or drinking ashore due to some health scare; even fraternizing with women was forbidden. Tours taken were Cairo, Pyramids, Alexandria Library (containing some of the oldest manuscripts remaining on earth), King Tut's Museum (gold artifacts for days, with even more submachine guns guarding it.)

Tony and I walked cautiously through Tut's Museum. Guards placed at every exit and window seemed overly preoccupied with us—downright staring.

"You have lipstick on? That's the third set of machine guns focused on us?" I asked.

"Girlfriend said I was a hot stud, senior year...if that counts? However, your point is taken."

"Tony, look around at the others...sunglasses. We're the only people wearing shades. That must be lighting their fuse."

"Hey, what can I say, 'Sun always shines...when you're cool,'" Tony recanted.

"Just control any urges you have in the 'five-finger discount' category, okay." Watching that movie *Midnight Express* (1978) is as close as I want to get to the prisons over here.

Lebanon had warring factions of Shiite and Sunni Muslim in a conflict instigated by Hezbollah troops which Iran was funding. President Reagan, eager to flex some of that muscle inherent to the US commander in chief, directed Forrestal circling about fifty miles offshore to conduct bombing runs on said factions. Results were devastating to neighborhoods of Lebanon. Jumping into a cauldron of continuous middle-eastern conflict based on religious differences has never worked out too well—Crusades—yes, that subject in school called history. Amazing what can be learned from others' mistakes.

People, incapable for multiple millennia, of explaining what science, at the time couldn't, formed religions. Zealots of one religion struck out at people worshiping another. So goes the ways of men—conquer and divide because interpretations of their religious doctrines tell them so. Sitting in the Philly shipyards months later, I would learn the ramifications of Reagan's desire. Hundreds of navy and marine personnel died in the barracks' bombing of Beirut. The retaliatory response was for the blood on the Gipper's hands; simply one dangerous zealot replying to another equally dangerous zealot.

Two months left on deployment, we pulled into Naples, Italy. Had duty first night in and remained on board. Tony, of course, poured salt in the wound.

"Is authentic Italian cuisine on your menu?" I ask.

"Out there somewhere, the daughter of Sophia Loren burns for me. I have only to find her."

"Take your romantic, Italian BS and hit the liberty boat. You find her…bring a picture to prove it."

Still awake at 1:00 a.m., I see Tony return with the fattest grin plastered upon his face. "I presume you're now Sophia Loren's new son-in-law."

"Nice guess, but you can do better."

"The pope granted you audience. You converted him to Southern Baptist."

The questioning expression on his face said it all. "What the hell?" he said as he threw a T-shirt over my head.

I grabbed the shirt. "Nice! You found a vendor selling high-quality Rolling Stones T-shirts."

"It's yours. Least I could do."

That stopped me; the previous grin was returning to his face. "Tony…what do you mean 'the least I co…?"

Tony's chin bobbing up and down, coaxing the realization. "No way."

"Yes way."

"Tonight? In Naples? You went to a Rolling Stones concert… here, in Italy?"

Tony's expression stamped validity to the claim. Stunned, I managed, "Did you know somehow, buy a ticket, then not tell me? Wait, don't answer that…I'd go to Leavenworth for murder."

Tony explained as soon as he walked off the docks, ticket scalpers were screaming, "Rolling Stones' tickets!" in English. The band had a concert performance in Naples that evening. No one on board had known about it.

"Look, I'm glad you got to see the Rolling Stones, but there's absolutely no way top brass on this ship didn't know before we arrived who was performing. Special Services would have made pre-arrival arrangements getting the news for sure. They kept a lid on it…closest the Forrestal would have come to a mutinous act on the cruise." I settled for Mount Vesuvius, Isle of Capri, and of course, Rome. Such were my priorities at the time.

Forrestal's liberty boat nudged the well-worn saltwater docks of Naples. Not lost upon me, the location, famous Italian port city at the foot of Vesuvius, was looming over the whole region. History that's occurred right here overwhelms the mind. Most of the mountain's top had been blown off in AD 79. Other bits and pieces, during smaller eruptions, over the next millennia. This huge mountain, minus its top of course, was a pre-planned visit Pete and I headed toward leaving the waterfront. Ports around the world have their own version of vendors; some honest, most not. Best left behind, we walked toward the city's train station. The schedule indicated the train that was taking us around to the mountain's other side would leave in five minutes—perfect timing. With multiple stops along the way, the slow-moving train lumbered upward while circumnavigating the mountain's base. We'd left the ship that morning looking for an authentic Italian meal with some shopping in mind at local artisan shops. A panoramic view from the train's window had me captured in some time warp within my mind. Roman Galleons anchored in the bay where the Forrestal currently lay.

"The next stop is an artisan village right on the cliffs overlooking the Mediterranean called Sorrento," Pete read off a brochure from the station back down the mountain.

"Let's see what it's like to walk without stepping over knee knockers. Maybe try out some authentic Italian pizza."

Perched on the side of Mount Vesuvius, Sorrento's citizens lived and worked within the most picturesque scenery I'd ever witnessed. Cobblestone streets led from the station between wood-working artisans' shops either side. Although having been at sea for weeks, I was somehow enamored; the view of the Mediterranean just ahead drew us deeper toward it. The vista everyone sees on Italian travel brochures lay at our feet. The restaurant straight ahead beckoned us within, yet both Pete and I pointed the waiter toward the open-air tables at the cliff's edge. Green ivy hung from the walls down toward the Mediterranean at least a couple hundred feet below. "This table will do, I been waiting for it my whole life," I told the old waiter.

"You're not the first American to say that," he gestured my way.

"We'd like a bottle of red wine, local stuff," I told him.

Looking over the retaining wall toward the drop below, Pete commented, "It's going to take a while to absorb this location…it is stunning."

"It'll get even better after a glass of wine."

Benito poured our wine and faded away. "Have you given any thought to what Hinson recounted?" Pete asked, his eyes locked on blue depths below the cliffs, as if searching for what Hinson had described.

I raised my glass of red local vino. "Here's to the balls it took for Hinson to admit what he saw. Unfortunately, he came to men he thought he could trust…his instructors, men he worked with…surely, they'd have his back…was thrown to the sharks." I drained my glass, instantly realizing the local wine carried a wallop. Standing for a little air, the sheer drop inches away, I sat back down. "Pete…researchers get new data continuously. One thing for sure, Uncle Sam, just like any other government will lie, cheat, or steal to get their hands on superior technology. Then never admit they got it."

"So you're on board with the alien, UFO possibility?" Pete asked.

"You really think that pyramid we just visited was to bury a pharaoh? Archeologists and trained researchers found evidence pyramids were built to transfer electricity, drawn outta the ground, into some usable energy. For whom and to do what? No way Egyptians were that advanced five thousand plus years ago without help."

"Maybe the Egyptians were at the top of their game," Pete stated.

"First thing popped in my mind when Hinson described a light rise out of the sea and disappear upward, Columbus' diary entry from 1492. He saw the same friggin' thing! Given the infinite number of star systems in the universe, not only is it possible, it's highly likely other advanced species have travelled to the third rock from this solar system's sun. We're attractive…blue water and green vegetation. Whatever they are, they're much more advanced than us. Obviously, they're capable of underwater travel. It would be to their benefit—very unlikely we'd detect it, so much of the seabed is never explored. One thing we should not take for granted is the unlimited possibilities that outer space has. Didn't you watch *Star Trek*?"

"Not religiously, as you seem to have."

"Look, Pete, you must pick and choose your own mental way of processing facts that are thrown at all of us every day. Most people could give a flying leap. There's a lot of bullshit to wade through… don't pay to be too gullible. Pick and choose your sources, then form your own opinion. Just don't gaff it off.

"Hinson was one strike away from pure shock. Obviously dazed. His words were upfront…unloading what he'd just witnessed. Hearing him and seeing his condition, I was stunned. Personally never believed it possible. Stuff just for movies. You're pretty much convinced?" Pete wondered.

"For whatever reason, aliens were probably coming here before we dominated over Neanderthals. They may have had a hand in our genetic makeup. If they needed free labor, there we were. Maybe a little chromosome manipulation could help their purposes with us. Ever wonder about all those half-men or half-animal characters described in literature or in paintings? I have."

"You are kidding, right?" Pete stopped, pouring his second glass of vino and looking at me.

"You sounded very similar to Senior Chief just now," I warned.

Pete said, "Touché!"

"Talked to a marine who was a tunnel runner in Nam. He came upon a half-lizard or half man in a cave—possibilities are unfathomable. Many of the people where I grew up could never wrap their mind around what we're discussing. Would never entertain the possibility. Even if 'little gray men' rang the doorbell, neighbors would think, 'more weirdos pushing Bibles.' Joining the navy, I swore I wouldn't be closed minded. Hey, Benito, can we order?"

At least twice within the western Mediterranean, we paused flight operations for a flight deck picnic—a day set aside at sea for the crew to have a break. Special Services Department would fly a musical band out to the ship with a few go-go girls. Mess cranks (cooks) threw burgers and dogs on the grill, even a couple of pissant Anchor beers per man that were strictly issued to only be consumed on the spot, of course.

This day, I'd lucked out when mail call put a shoebox-size parcel in my hand. The luck of this arriving that day astounded me. What was inside? A pre-arranged order I'd written the wife to send my way a month or so before. Six cans of pre-mixed whiskey sours—what luck. Prior to the band striking up, I sat in my bunk, curtains drawn, drinking three of said cans. Forty-five minutes later, after carefully descending from the top rack, full sails blowing in the wind, I was on my way up to the well-deserved hoedown.

Short of the steel-deck picnic by one last ladder, I realized someone in an officer's khaki uniform was descending—damn. Okay, I'd back away, let this officer have a wide berth and be on his merry way. Of the thousands of friggin' people on the ship, down the ladder scampers the ship's executive officer—the badass in charge of dealing out punishment during XO's mast for fuckups. Mother of God! What felt like the displacement of internal organs was surely held in check by the slamming of the doors to the lower orifice. I backed up even further, held my breath, and smiled. He recognized me from CATCC and held out his hand to shake mine. What the? Surely not a coup-de-gras takedown; my inebriated mind was somehow racing through such possibilities. He was proud actually; pleased with the work we'd done so far. With as little hesitation I could muster, I held my ground, bent slightly at the waist with an outstretched hand, not saying a word. He continued descending while I slowly climbed the ladder upward. What were the odds? Tabulating such seemed too monumental, as shit faced as I was.

Our last port of call was Benidorm, on the Spanish coast. We anchored at least a mile from the beach which looked teeming with activity for this time of year. As the anchor and chain sank, our spirits lifted. Observing a slow parade of what looked like pedal boats heading toward the ship, sailors on the flight deck, myself included, took notice. Benidorm had become a popular mecca for European tourists seeking vacation from the Lapland and northern regions beyond. I began whistling a favorite Beach Boys tune from "Good Vibrations" (1966) beginning a slow crawl up my spine. As the parade, slowly heading our way, came into clearer view—our eyes surely deceived us. At least a dozen paddle boats began circling our huge ship powered by the leg muscles of topless, European women promoting, the easiest way they could on-the-spur, relations with the USA.

From our view at the bar, we sipped our glass of beer flavored with lemon juice, a first for me, and munched on olives where I'd normally find peanuts. Located on the beach, this bar's glass windows amply displayed the marvelous nature found on that beach on all forms. Turns out razor blades in that neck of the woods are scarce or some women aren't concerned with armpit hair; I don't know, just saying, every rose has it thorns.

CV-59 left Benidorm heading toward Gibraltar. Senior Chief passed the word that AC3 Hinson was onboard a C-131 navy transport aircraft on final to Jacksonville Naval Air Station. As of this time, undetermined causes are responsible for the aircraft's crash directly into the St. John's River, all dead.

Don't recall getting from CATCC to the fantail at the aft end of the ship, looking out to sea with the ship's wake spreading out in the distance; some sailor had hold of my shoulder, asking why I was screaming.

Entering the Atlantic on our home leg, Poseidon got his bowels in an uproar. A storm whipped up the Atlantic pummeling 40 ft. waves over the bow. Others of the crew not immune to sea sickness had a "blow-chunks festival" any and everywhere. Squads of sailors patrolled the passageways cleaning up lakes of vomit. Belts were used to secure one's body into their rack during attempts at sleeping. Horrendous situation as it was, the smaller ships supporting CV-59 all around us had it much worse. Somehow those huge waves spared them a grave on the seafloor during the three-day chum-soup circus.

Philadelphia Naval Shipyard— January 1983

Shipyard schedules must be met. The Forrestal had a date in Philadelphia beginning in January for a stripped-down overhaul. Most everyone would be transferred to other ships, holding only a skeleton crew aboard for the transit north then to work the overhaul—intensive labor. I was asked to stay on to supervise the installation of new radar equipment for ATC; sea duty in Philadelphia, duh!

At some point, people in training for driving a car must tackle the parallel parking hurdle. Substitute the automobile with an aircraft carrier pulling up to an awaiting dock. One of the most meticulous maneuvers I've ever observed. Boatmanship to the extreme. Every opportunity available, I had a first-row seat. From this perch, I prepared for another demonstration. After one month of homeport stay post Indian Ocean cruise, the ship headed north along the seaboard, making the turn into the Delaware River. I took in the lights of Philadelphia, Pennsylvania, on the left and Trenton, New Jersey on the right. These lights, from skyscrapers in both mega cities, cast a colorful, reflecting sheen on the existing shroud of blowing snow associated with an ongoing New England clipper. Conditions that only added to the monumental task of parking this floating hunk of steel in a flooded dry dock within the Philadelphia Naval Shipyard. The low base sound of a foghorn helped orient the ship's helmsman. Waters from the Delaware River, as well as assisting tugboats, kept the massive hulk buoyant during the evolution.

Clutching my peacoat over the thickest uniform I had, my dress blues, I watched from the flight deck's edge as boatswain mates secured the ship's mooring lines onto a bustling dock below. Snow had begun falling only an hour prior to our arrival on Friday evening, yet a deep whiteness blanketed every surface visible. Whenever a ship is moored, a descending perpendicular ladder is attached to the dock for access to and from the ship called the brow. This position must be manned 24-7 by a sailor, with a marine guard, on a four-hour rotating basis. How I was the first sailor to man this brow, now linking the Forrestal to the City of Brotherly Love, was my usual par for the course. Checking oncoming personnel's credentials, which may or may not allow their access to the ship, was the duty involved. Popping salutes with frozen appendages could not be neglected in the subfreezing weather. From Friday p.m. to Sunday a.m., Philly recorded twenty-three inches of snow fall. Had the ship overshot the correct inlet—pulled into Greenland? My introduction to life above the Mason-Dixon Line obviously created this now shared memory. Within a month and road weary for the second move in eighteen months, I returned to Florida and moved the family north to Philadelphia; we were together and trying to keep it that way.

This mission, detached from typical frontline defense, was necessary to maintain the ship's integrity in future deployments. As challenging as each day at sea had been, preference given I'd go ahead and complete eighteen remaining months of my sea duty here in the shipyard, thank you. Dog-day labor, as it would turn out to be; another way of saying shipyard workers have the nastiest, greasiest, stress-intensified work environment within a clouded mist of metal-grinded air I've ever participated in. Absolutely everything was removed whether bolted down or not. Only steel bulkheads and deck were left to be needle gunned and sanded down.

Operations Department tagged me to coordinate and supervise daily job details within our spaces. These "jobs" required a skillset I knew I must develop, like pronto. Occasionally, a trip down below was required into the dry dock itself, below the Forrestal. The ship sat on gigantic wooden blocks placed every fifty feet or so. Most people have seen a picture or film clip of an aircraft carrier, noting the immense size. Walking on the bottom of a dry dock after the Delaware River had been drained, the bottom of this monstrosity suspended just over your hardhat, was just spooky. Upward of five thousand sailors banking on watertight integrity during our Indian Ocean cruise came to mind, looking up at giant propellers at the ships aft.

Directly adjacent the dry dock, a two-story building provided office space for management of maintenance details on the ship next door. During the cold winter, many sailors found any excuse possible to avoid work details in the sharp temperatures. A head (restroom) break, chief among them. To accommodate the number of sailors, this office building had a very large head with a dozen enclosed toilets all in a row. Sailors, waiting their turn for their only private space in an eight-hour shift, stood in a lengthy line no more than ten feet in front of and parallel to the dozen toilets.

Once inside this temporary mecca from work, along with the stench of its original purpose, sailors decided to take out personal grievances using graffiti. Their target, 99 percent of the time, was the XO. Yes, the same khaki-clad judge, jury, and executioner I'd encountered climbing to a steel-deck hootenanny months before. His reputation, indelibly ensconced upon the walls of a dozen meccas all in a row, surely wasn't the epitaph he was banking on in front of St. Peter at the Golden Gate. Made aware of his dastardly earned accolades, the XO, under his hardhat, turned the corner into operations. "Petty Officer Harper, this week's schedule has no room in it, yet somehow, you're going to find enough. Main head, second deck, have those toilet enclosures painted over by tomorrow morning."

"Yes, sir." Schedule was altered. The XO smiled. I smiled. Next morning, the situation was addressed at muster, warnings issued, blah, blah, blah. Problem solved, done deal. "Get your personal business taken care of, get back to grinding metal." Nah, didn't happen. People with dull axes to grind will react, given anonymity, within an enclosure providing cover. Sailors viewed this move as a brand-new canvas for more artwork with accompanying details. Chasing a likely culprit would be an extensive project leading to rabbit holes the XO, more than likely, wanted to avoid.

After his weekly inspection, the XO approached my desk as I popped to attention. His crystal blue eyes, now cloudy, with an absolute chance of imminent hellfire. Mind retro-flashed for a millisecond; taking it up the shorts in front of a Filipino master chief back in the Philippines.

The tip of XO's nose aligned no more than eight inches from my own—his choice not mine. Breath indicated whatever he'd had for breakfast wasn't agreeing with him. "Harper, do people in your department have something against me?"

"Damned if you do, damned if you don't" quicksand traps, habitually lurked around this individual. How in hell was I gonna tell Judge Roy Bean, practically twirling a hangman's noose in my face, something semi-honest. His method of soliciting—perhaps a slip of my tongue was his target, all for something he was already aware.

"Sir, most everyone experiences attacks of animosity from others, some…more than others. We try to deal with it or accept it and move on."

"Harper, as I see it…you, yourself have one remedy to accept. I'll check tomorrow morning if we're on the same page."

XOs always have the last laugh. That evening after work, a dozen forced volunteers removed all enclosures surrounding each toilet, leaving only the row of porcelain bowls. The line of awaiting sailors, now each in their own version of a nature's call, would wait, as if in front of a stage at jazz fest, 10 ft. away from occupied toilets in full exposure. All the edible delights Philadelphia was known for—pretzels, Philadelphia cheesesteak, and turkey and ham subs didn't help. Whatever condition your stomach decided to send your way after that day, may as well have been the headlines in the *Philadelphia Enquirer*. Each day's work-completion rate picked up rapidly for some reason.

Generally avoided large cities except passing through, knowing the negative aspects of concrete jungles. Philadelphia was the exception; couldn't get enough. From ethnic cuisine, historical content, sports venues, great nightclub scenes, and involvement in relevant issues, this place was happening. It wasn't because I'd spent the last seven months sleeping in a tight berthing compartment with thirty-some odd sailors, who usually needed a good bath. Benjamin

Franklin started this place humming some 225 years ago. It's still ticking. "Philadelphia Freedom" Elton John (1975).

History fascinates the imagination, often repeating itself with the steady progression of new characters, challenging the same plot over and over. The whole Philadelphia area has been simmering in a rich historical broth for centuries; the children now had a chance to sup from that ladle. The Poconos, Hershey Park, Allentown's Great Adventure, Independence Hall, Bucks County KOA campground, Washington DC's monuments, all and more kept us busy for eighteen months. Combination of a new phenomenon called MTV and an extra fifteen pounds added on from the famed Philly cheesesteak later, I knew I could really get use to this place. Along with such a menu, the marital relationship slowly ascended from a low valley to the point where our last pregnancy began.

The family and I left the parking lot behind in DC, walking toward a memorial unlike all others in the city. Imbedded in the lush grass, as if protruding from it, was the Vietnam Memorial. I knew a couple names from my hometown in Louisiana would be there. I wanted the children to ponder the concept of sacrifice for one's country. Beautiful black monument, permanently announcing with pride and honor the names of those who gave their last full measure during the Vietnam War.

This memorial had visitors in uniform, partial uniforms, and those like us in civilian attire. People were placing flowers and mementos; others sobbing; some leaning on the memorial, a hand touching all that was left of a loved one, their name. We turned around at the end, retracing our steps, a somber feeling controlling the environment.

Passing a male figure, hair beyond his shoulders, do-rag over his head, my eyes landed on a tattoo. The unique design was one I'd observed before. We strolled on a couple minutes, mind racing through the thousands of tattoos I'd seen on countless sailors. Like a slot machine, the dials of memory spools stopped; it wasn't a sailor but a marine: Gunny Sergent Birdwell from the Astro Club above Magsaysay Boulevard in Olongapo, Philippines. I turned around heading back toward this figure. Beard covering most of his face, I just wasn't sure. Tattoo was in the right place though. Approaching the lone figure leaning against the wall his hand over someone's name, I addressed him. "Excuse me, would you happen to be Gunny Sergent Birdwell?" As his head turned, I remembered the faraway look he'd had in his eyes before, and it was still there. Those eyes were now glazed over with moisture indicating to me I'd interrupted a special moment for him. "I'm so sorry, I see now is not a good time to talk."

"Do I know you?"

"Once…for a couple hours anyway. We met in a club in the PI about, hmm…seven years ago."

He turned to face me when I noticed part of his ear missing. "Bar in the PI? You really think I could remember that?"

"You described your work down in the tunnels during some missions in the highlands."

That locked his eyes with mine. As he turned toward a nearby bench, I could see he was now using a prosthetic arm from the right elbow down. He and I sat with my family out of earshot.

"Sorry, I can't recall…but you obviously know me."

"You didn't have that the last time we talked," I said pointing to his prosthetic.

"Marines told me I'd given enough blood for the cause and sent me packing. I bitched and moaned, really had no choice."

"You come to the wall often?" I asked.

"Still undergoing physical therapy at Walter Reed."

"Did that happen in a tunnel exploration?"

"A couple years after PI, around '78…volunteered for a clandestine operation going in country. Good intel at the time, had a prisoner-of-war camp located in the same area of the cave…the one I had to return to."

Sitting on a bench, of all places, in front of the Vietnam Memorial wasn't a good place to bring it up, but the elephant parading through my mind, the source of more than one nightmare over the years since I'd heard it from this man's mouth couldn't be ignored. Odds were I'd never see the man again. "Tell me, Birdwell, did you ever confront…lizard man again?"

His eyes took on a look of warning; I may have just stepped in a steaming pile, but I remembered; he was reliving his memory. Eventually he said, "You must've kept buying San Miguel, very few people know about that. During reconnaissance of the area searching for the POW camp, I, and my backup, went in. Reentering the opening, we stayed together prepared for battle. With flashlights this time, we penetrated deeper. Around eighty feet in, we were ambushed by two of 'em. Mangled my arm, took a chunk of my ear...my assistant pulled me out...owe that man my life."

Taken aback by what I'd just heard, I literally had to pull my wits together to ask the question, "Birdwell, did you make a kill that day?"

Eyes, like the Holy Bible's Old Testament on my grandma's nightstand, were wide open for all to read. "You'll never hear that come from my lips," he said, cueing in a deja vu moment.

As he made his way along the memorial, my eyes landed on the belt he was wearing, the sheath holding his bowie knife, and of course, his do-rag—all were made of lizard skin.

Time for rotation nearing, I requested and got orders to Naval Air Station Corpus Christi for its highly valued air traffic intensity. One big plus with this move was my old college pal Eric, who worked in the area.

Naval Air Station Corpus Christi, Texas—1984

Trainee pilots for the navy got behind the stick initially at NAS Pensacola. Those with promise were sent to Corpus Christi to learn flying technique, navigation, mostly how to survive. Starting out green, pilots learned quickly—died trying or washed out. ATC rules conformed to both USN and FAA regs; we enforced them or people flying could, very well, not return alive. Within a week of arrival, I was tasked as section leader of fourteen controllers, some qualified at all positions, others in training as was I. Challenges approached from all angles; where to step and not overstep authority, especially in a training status while absorbing the local environment, all the while, directing members of the section and writing their evaluations.

A natural seaside bay on the western shores of the Gulf of Mexico, Corpus Christi's waters are somewhat shielded from the open gulf by a lengthy finger island called Padre Island. Outside the city, thickets of mesquite abound. Spohn Hospital delivered our second daughter. This beautiful baby girl was the cherry on top of the best three years I had in the navy. "True Colors" Cyndi Lauper (1986). Eric and I fished for speckled trout and redfish. Padre Island Beach often served as a playground where vehicles were allowed and sand dunes abound. Dangers prowled beyond the surf; a young teen girl running out of waist-high waves clutching what remained of a bloody arm from a shark's bite. Eric observed my two sons going under on their last breath, thankfully with the right person right time. Eric saved them from Padre Island surf. Best friends forever!

Training on a radar advisory position called "seagull" with ten to fifteen flights on my frequency, a flight of two T-34s checked in over the gulf heading back to base. Establishing radar contact, I turned them for a direct vector toward home. Ten miles away, a primary target popped on screen with no altitude display nor radio contact; its direction of flight could intersect with the two 34s, but I'd return to this situation in due time. As the primary target approached five miles distance on an intersecting course with the 34s, the pilots reported bad visibility, unable to spot the traffic call. The primary-target-only aircraft was "possibly" high over our airspace and no factor inbound to Corpus Christi's civilian airport. Yet the distance diminishing between, I pointed out the target to the 34s each mile, including, "Less than a mile, report traffic in sight." The 34 pilots didn't observe the small aircraft until it was upon them at the same altitude. Prepared, a last-second maneuver avoided a midair collision. The pilots filed a near-miss report along with a written "atta-boy" to my command. In this business, then for twelve years, last-minute saves were more common than the navy wanted publicized. Here, where pilots were taught rules save lives and shortcuts mean mistakes, controllers kept vigil.

Mid-eighties under President Reagan brought ample funding for defense, translating into more pilot training and ultimately heavier air traffic for us. Facility qualified and section leader for a year, an old friend from both Cubi Point and CV-59, AC1 Allen, and I, became day and eve tower supervisors. Idle minutes at work did not exist. The approach end of a main runway was a mile and a half from where air traffic controllers stood in the control tower. Add one to three miles for the final approach phase of flight when wheels must be down and locked. Tower observers needed more than a pilot's word; couldn't trust 'em. We had to visually confirm during daylight hours that wheels were in fact down. Nighttime required an on-sight wheels watch in a shack about 500 ft. from the approach end. If they observed no wheels on a passing aircraft, they triggered a toggle switch that ignites wave-off flares on either side of the approach end. Imagine that job; anything longer than a blink, you could miss the one aircraft flying by wheels up—you've blown it. Binocular verification of wheels-down reports prior to landing was an absolute. The lack of experience, prevalent in these new-to-the-stick aviators, hanging over our head.

One morning, pulling up to the approach light area for the active runway in the duty pickup, I was told by the tower, "Hold short," on my FM handheld radio. It was their response to my call for access onto the duty runway for a light check. From a right base, behind my position, a flight of two T-2s had been cleared for landing. I turn my head looking out the truck cab's back window; one of the T-2s has his tailhook down. If he was making an arrested landing in the arresting gear, I hadn't heard any chatter on the FM radio concerning it. I called the tower on the FM radio, "Tower, for your info, one of your T-2s has his hook down?"

"Ops 1, Tower. Roger."

The tower questioned the pilot of his intentions. He was unaware his tailhook was even down. The flight was waved off from landing for another pass with just wheels down. Had his aircraft engaged the arresting gear without the pilot's intention; well, my imagination warned me not to dwell.

I called the fourteen air traffic controllers within section two to attention during fall in. Just prior to commencing the day watch, I read pertinent items off the NAS Corpus Plan of the Day then gave a brief check of uniforms.

"Airman Pagano, did you use a Brillo-pad on those shoes?"

"No, sir," Pagano replied.

"Airman Pagano, do not refer to me as sir, that's for officers. I'm your section leader."

"Right."

"Go into the radar room, get the shoe polish kit, and put a shine on those clodhoppers now." My vision's edge picked up the next sailor, "Good morning, Petty Officer Cloud." He'd been escorted from the sheriff's department with his wife to the front gate under guard from fear of death threats about a month ago. Navy brought them on board and put them into available housing. Cloud had been held in custody by local authorities until initial investigation into possible murder charges cleared him of any wrongdoing.

Three blocks outside the main gate sat a section of low-rent housing, which suited Cloud and his wife's budget when they'd moved into the area four months prior. Cloud initially believed the surrounding houses were vacant until three weeks later; the Bandito Motorcycle Gang returned to their winter home and hangout. Cloud's wife was worried. Danger surrounded them. She knew her husband could take care of himself, but she was still vulnerable. Were the doors and windows secure? Within the week, Cloud had shot and killed an intruder in their home—a member of the Bandito Motorcycle Gang.

Next in line, I see Faulk, a prankster to the nth degree. Last month, he'd taken a road trip through the Big Bend area of Texas. Near sunset, he observed numbers of tarantula spiders crossing the paved road, nightmarish as it sounds. Faulk stopped, captured one of the spiders in some container, and continued back to Corpus Christi. The plan he'd hatched was a continuation of an ongoing tit-for-tat game, of which I was unaware, between himself and PO Boaz, also in the section.

Majority of controllers bring their lunch to work. Time constraints with work and fast-food prices on our salary didn't constitute good money management. PO Faulk transferred the tarantula from his container into Boaz' lunch box sitting next to the refrigerator in the breakroom. As lunch time neared, Faulk waited for Boaz to eat his lunch. Working in the radar room, I was giving a precision radar approach to an A-4 Skyhawk on a two-mile final to the runway. Thankfully, my transmitter wasn't keyed as a high-pitched scream penetrated the whole building. I couldn't respond. Finally on the A-4's rollout, I switched the jet to tower's frequency.

Boaz had sat down at a table in the breakroom. Opening his lunch box, the tarantula, bigger than a man's open hand with fingers extended, jumped onto the table, and scampered under a nearby sofa. Boaz went batshit berserk, screaming louder than a flock of black crows, ran outside, and wouldn't return. Beside himself, Faulk knew his prank couldn't be topped. I ordered Faulk to capture the spider and put it in his vehicle to dispose of after work. I lassoed Boaz from hysteria and brought him back in the breakroom. "This game ends now. If you two ten-year-olds want to grow up and join the adults in the control room…it starts now. Boaz, next two eve watches you will advise Petty Officer Faulk of any meal of your choosing under five dollars, to which he will have delivered to you at work."

Back at muster, I said, "Petty Officer Faulk, you're in the military not a member of ZZ Top. Soon as muster is over, head over to the base barber shop when it opens at 8:00 a.m., clear?"

"Petty Officer Harper, those barbers will see my hair and start drooling. I regularly go to a salon out the main gate, they don't open till 0900."

"When Lieutenant Commander Salerno walks in at 0800 and sees your golden locks, he'll come looking for who allowed you to cultivate them. Now, I could tell him you promised to go to your 'salon' by 0900…*not gonna happen*! 0800 base barber, let's see some white sidewalls this time."

"Section 2, at ease. The inbound board in base operations has a C-5 Galaxy inbound around ten hundred this morning, other than that, looks like a typical day. Corrello, I'm expecting a PAR (precision approach radar) qualification recommendation on you this afternoon. Everyone, check the schedule for your work assignments. Section 2, atten-hut! Dismissed."

Along with a coast guard detachment on station running search and rescue operations for this region, NAS Corpus Christi also had a US Army detachment with their own hangar which conducted maintenance on vast numbers of helicopters. The US Air Force brought the ailing army copters to our detachment on their monster load hauler of an aircraft, the C-5 Galaxy. Trips into our station for this purpose normally occurred monthly.

The air station sits on reacclimated beach front property where Corpus Christi Bay's entrance to the Gulf of Mexico begins. Not the stalwart bedrock on which foundations would optimally be secured. Shifting sands although compacted underground still tend to shift. See where this is going?

Signed on as tower supervisor, I checked with Corpus Approach Control on the position of the inbound C-5. "Corpus approach, navy tower. You have a posit on a C-5 inbound our house?"

"Twenty miles northeast for a TACAN approach, WW."

"Roger."

I called flight support to position a follow-me truck for guiding the C-5 to parking. The sheer weight of an empty Galaxy aircraft is tremendous. Add a dozen to eighteen helicopters as cargo and hear the scales ring the bell every time. Before the procedure of bringing in these ailing helos for a tune up began, the whole scenario of weight limits requiring stress tests had occurred. Knowing the unreliability of shifting sands as a support base, regular tests were conducted on the specific path heavy aircraft would be taking to their sight of off-loading.

"Navy Corpus, MAC588 Heavy clearing the runway for parking."

"MAC588 Heavy, follow-me control, taxi to parking," Navy Corpus ground controller responded.

"Roger."

The hangar where the offload would occur had multiple vehicles staged to commence the procedure when cleared to begin. Normal operations continued with a flight of two T-44s inbound for an overhead approach into an existing pattern with two aircraft. Essentially complete from our standpoint, I still observed the C-5 slowly making its final positioning on the ramp now under a lineman's direction. Year after year of working on every type aircraft the navy used, I lingered over the immensity of this C-5 in contrast to the pilot training aircraft the navy utilized. Without warning, the whole port (left) side of the Galaxy collapsed at least six to seven feet. Its port landing gear had crushed through the ramp. I jumped across the tower cab and grabbed the crash phone. "Crash, crash, crash…C-5 Galaxy port main mount has collapsed through the ramp surface at the unloading sight. Port wingtip is wedged on the ramp surface, fuel leak observed." We had a major problem with the leaking fuel.

"MAC588 Heavy, tower observes a fuel leak under your port wing, crash-fire enroute. Say your fuel state and how many personnel on board," Simmons inquired from ground control.

"Twenty thousand pounds in the port wing and eight crew members ready at any moment to vacate soon as I get this whale put to rest and crash captain gives the okay."

"Roger."

I grab the FM microphone "Crash captain, navy tower. C5's port wing has twenty thousand pounds of fuel, eight crew, a full load of helos, and the pilots shutting down engines. Your command… advise when crew can deploy."

"Navy Tower, I'll get back to you ASAP."

Tower continued operating flights in and out. I watched the fuel leak increase; had the C-5's load of onboard helos shifted, increasing the pressure on the wing? The fuel spill was puddling up on the ramp. Firemen deployed portable boundaries to hopefully contain it from spreading. Empty drums were being brought from the hangar. Once in place, the fuel leak could be collected. The whole area was cleared of non-essential personnel. Days like this gave credence to emergency personnel operating in a situation which, at any second, could barbecue all within the hazardous zone. Those guys do a great job, but I'm glad I chose the job I did.

"Navy Tower, Crash Captain. Advise the aircrew to digress forward of the aircraft."

The aircrew left the scene safely, allowing emergency personnel to handle the mess. Fuel drained from the busted wing tank into continuous barrels for two hours while what had spilled on the ramp was suctioned up. The aircraft was a different story. It sat for two days waiting for a crane with enough lift capacity to be hauled in. Woe be unto shifting sands.

The age of eight to ten years old, during my childhood, brought out hair-raising events. Insane exploits I pulled off surely could never be rivalled. Wrong; the two boys growing up in my household had it baked in. The housing area we lived in on base was isolated from others living in newer housing. Surrounded by empty dwellings, the two obviously treated housing units and carports as playground objects to climb on when I was conveniently at work. Turning into housing, I see two kids running over the roof of an empty unit, too far to identify, but my boys? No doubt. I'd lived the days of boredom as a kid, launching off into wild schemes to cure the feeling. I saw the same angst in these young squirts—only remedy was providing a safe, alternative, constant supervision and communication. I had made this choice ten years before and was determined to see it through. Despite the hard knocks they would inevitably encounter, remaining within civil-boundary lines was my goal. Not always an easy task, the salve I applied for my comfort was of course Bruce Hornsby, ZZ Top, Don Henley, Peter Gabriel, SRV, and the Cult helped weave each day's fabric into the next.

Airman Apprentice Juneau had joined the navy practically under duress. Pressure had been applied by the district judge back in Ohio, for minor theft. Juvenile lockup in an overflowing detention center or pass along the buck to Uncle Sam—a no-brainer for the judge, however, a win-win for Juneau. He'd be practically beating the rap by riding the system, all the while on a path to greener fields. Now, four months later, Juneau found himself detailed to NAS Corpus Christi transit line. The job required enough knowledge about the various types of naval aircraft to guide the taxiing aircraft to a parking spot and chock the aircraft's wheels, inserting locking pins when required. Training for this job was an absolute necessity, yet Juneau's lack of inspiration concerned his supervisor. Too many dangers lurked around aircraft engines, both jet and propeller driven, shutting down or turning up.

"I've been bailing you out this whole week, Juneau. Procedures are written covering everything we must do in this job. I've watched you 'wingin' it,' skipping the correct sequence while assisting the pilot during shutdown. The study material you were given upon check-in probably hasn't left your locker. It isn't for wiping your ass with."

Airman Apprentice Juneau knew who's face he loved to wipe his ass with, but responded, "Boss, I was studying through section IV until late last night." Juneau knew, as the supervisor suspected, the material had sat in his locker for two weeks untouched. He would now have to somehow sneak the material from his locker unseen when the shift was over.

SCUTTLEBUTT

Airman Lafleur sat quietly on the porcelain throne, located in the "head" of his barrack's room he shared with Airman Apprentice Juneau. The chow hall's version of pork chop suey, causing a series of internal combustion flare-ups in Lafleur's gut, had prompted a dash for his own personal "head"—well semiprivate. As of two weeks ago, he had a different roommate. Five minutes with the guy, Lafleur knew he'd be keeping his locker secured, hiding anything of value. All alone upon entering, he relished the solitude to relieve himself.

Five minutes later, still perched on the toilet in relaxed bliss, Lafleur hears the room door open, electing to remain quiet. Juneau entered the door to his barrack's room, throwing his study material on his rack before going to take a leak. Stopping short of the door to the head, he realized he was alone. He now had the opportunity to check out what he'd seen his roommate stash away under his mattress. Lifting it up, he smiled, recognizing an envelope from the Navy Federal Credit Union with the corner of green money bills exposed. Juneau reached for the envelope as Airman Lafleur exited the head to see his mattress upturned.

"WTF!" Lafleur yelled. "You lift that green, you'll have to get past me." Juneau dropped the mattress empty handed, surprised and slack jawed.

The threat was nothing to whistle Dixie to. Lafleur had a good sixty pounds of muscle, acquired with daily workouts at the base gym, over Juneau. Now back against his own rack, Juneau shifted to a practiced version of his smile of innocence. "I saw you place something there, I was just curious that's all… I swear."

"Stay on your side of the room. Touch anything that's mine, I'll break your arms and legs. Throw you in the bay for sharks. Now, until I'm ready to move it, that money stays where it is…all $180 of it. You want to feed the sharks, Juneau?"

"Of course not, you've misunderstood me," Juneau said leaving the room. He'd been unable to take the heat given off from Lafleur's sincerity, his eyes driving the threat home. Would he be reported to security? Would Lafleur retaliate out of spite? He had stupidly resorted to his old ways, now his ass was in the fire again. He'd have to worry about this later after his shift at the transit line.

Working in the tower that late afternoon, I noticed the inbound board indicated a four-engine Lockheed Electra, or P-3 as the navy referred to them, inbound for a gas and go. It's a common aircraft utilized for patrolling the seas by dropping sonar buoys in the ocean which can detect submarine movement. However, NAS Corpus Christi is not a typical air station the P-3 utilizes.

Corpus Approach buzzed the inbound line in the control tower with a P-3 twenty-two miles south or southwest for a TACAN approach to our duty runway. Utilizing the TACAN's radials projected from the ground equipment, the P-3's onboard receiver can guide the aircraft to the runway. Reporting in, the P-3 was given a clearance to land. The flight data operator in the tower called the transit line telling them an inbound P-3 was wanting a gas and go. The P-3 switched to ground control frequency then proceeded to parking.

Grabbing his own gear, the transit supervisor told Juneau, "You haven't picked up one study guide since coming on watch. Where is it? Did you go over it? Procedures to service aircraft uncommon to our transit line were covered in the study material."

"Sure, boss, I studied it like you ordered," Juneau lied now, remembering throwing it on his rack unread.

"Grab your gear, a four-engine turboprop is wanting services. We'll see how much you retained from that study material. Let's go!"

The traffic in my tower bounce pattern consisted to two T-44s practicing touch-and-go approaches. The ground controller and I observed the larger P-3 park at the T-line under the guidance of the daily supervisor. His assistant was to the side of the four-engine aircraft stationed near fire bottles, if needed. A working team on any airport had to utilize hand signals between each other due to the abundant aircraft noise. In place, the supervisor gave Juneau the signal to put the wooden chocks fore and aft of the wheels. Juneau glared back at the supervisor as if he just been "flipped off," having no idea what the hand signal meant. Impatiently waiting, the supervisor shook his head and pointed at the chocks.

Overwhelmed with the size of this huge turboprop, Juneau felt as if his teeth were vibrating. He noticed the supervisor pointing at something, seemingly waiting for him to comply. *Of course, I need to chock the wheels*, he remembered.

The current pattern work I had been involved with slowed to zero as the T-44s made a full stop and switched to ground control. The transient line is close enough to the tower that the four engines of the P-3 created noise pollution through our thick windowpanes. I stood up to see how much longer before he began shutting down. The transient line assistant stood up from placing chocks at the nose wheel. The P-3's engines began winding down. A red mist suddenly appeared around engine number two next to the cabin of the P-3. Parts of the assistant's body flew into the air. The supervisor began running the 25 feet toward the scene when Juneau's body, from the waist down only, fell immediately in front of the supervisor. Gagging from the spectacle, I turned and grabbed the crash phone, alerting medical to send an ambulance. Unsaid, I knew they would need a large shovel.

Investigation detailed Juneau's state of mind prior to the incident. Airmen Lafleur told of the situation at the barracks prior to the incident. Transient line supervisor was held accountable for safety violations since Juneau's PQS or personnel qualifications weren't sufficient for him to have been doing the job that killed him.

Six months prior to leaving Texas, I took the written exam for chief controller, a burdensome annual event, now my fifth time. Promotion in ATC happened, not when a candidate warranted such but when the USN needed a promoted person. Of the half-dozen local candidates, ATC administration backed one with zeal, one whose "attaboy" had turned into a Navy Achievement Medal warranting recognition. Told outright by the office, "If advanced, I'd get sea duty orders back to a ship." This news totally washed through the home front like thunderstorms on Fat Tuesday. I began making clandestine calls to the landlocked branch of the navy called TAR. This small segment of active-duty sailors trains naval reservists. My switchover could guarantee no sea duty.

Picked up chief, switched to the TAR branch, and got orders back to New Orleans. Blatant, total alienation from ATC in Corpus—in their eyes, I was a turncoat. I had stood up for myself and my family instead of the needs of the regular navy. My kids, by now, required a father figure present, not on a ship at sea. "That's Just the Way It Is," Bruce Hornsby (1986). I knew then Belle Chasse, Louisiana is where I'd retire with twenty years, giving the kids a familiar high school they deserved.

NAS New Orleans, Louisiana— September 1987

The chief's set of khakis, with anchors on the collar, ushered me through the door to administration. For fifteen years, I'd worked around the ATC office conforming to their regimen. I'd always remained clear of office inner dynamics, where personalities therein hashed out written instruction on a daily basis. Amidst this challenge, I requested and received the position of tower chief.

Glad to move down to the office arena from the tower, Chief Leblanc was a Louisiana native like myself. Fortunately for me, I had avoided whatever swamp Leblanc had crawled out of to join the land of the living. The reoccurring, mean-tooth grin Leblanc sported seemed akin to the gator which hung out around the base golf course visible on the daily drive to work. Until I could figure the guy out, attempts at avoiding Leblanc never succeeded—the housing unit we were assigned was right next door for God's sake. In his infinite wisdom, the division officer assigned Chief Leblanc as my sponsor while I went through the initiation process for navy chief; as nostalgic a period of bliss, gathering reflective memories, as enduring a bout of shingles. As with life, I sucked it up, remembering George Harrison's "All Things Must Pass" (1970).

A wealth of technique from various tower chiefs over the previous fifteen years, gave ample methods from which I gleaned a path to operate. Passing along guidance in a constructive manner, hopefully instilling confidence in a controller's ability to manage NAS New Orleans' typical pattern: F-15s intermixed with P-3s and C-130s at 1,500 feet. Underneath, below 500 feet, petroleum helicopters and civilian float planes transited with tower's permission, toward oil rigs in the Gulf of Mexico. Straight-in flights, whether radar controlled or instrument approach, were a factor for sequencing across the runway's threshold. After completing the training program, whoever demonstrated their control of the airport traffic, all factors above considered, received a tower ticket. I was told I succeeded. Determined ones found that niche, developed their abilities, undoubtedly reaping the rewards of self-satisfaction.

After weeks of playing with our minds, navy chiefs on the base decided initiation day was set at the Chief's Club. Approximately ten of us were going through the day-long process. The penning ceremony, where the anchors were attached to our collar, would follow. Torture ensued. A couple of dastardly requirements were eating through a grizzly concoction of raunchy edibles in a hog trough with hands tied behind our backs while on our knees trying to dig our collar anchors from the bottom with our teeth. We sat on an electrified commode seat. Oh, happy days! Chief Leblanc's grin greeted my misery throughout the process.

In addition to being an active naval air station, NAS New Orleans was a training base for navy reservists referred to as "weekend warriors." This concept provided an arena where once a month, reservists from the southern region of the US converged in Belle Chasse, Louisiana for training at whatever job they'd volunteered for in uniform and within military guideline. Our job was to train them to be ready for that job when they were called up for duty. Arriving on Friday evening, hundreds would fly from Houston on navy transports. The approximate number of reservists inbound had to be known to coordinate for busing the arriving personnel from the ramp to berthing so two full days over the weekend could be utilized for training.

Weather in the New Orleans area on one Friday afternoon was typically humid with an increasing chance of storms in the early evening. Reserve weekend and once again operations duty officer until Saturday a.m. The flight schedule was typically moderate to heavy, slowly winding down after sunset. The reservists transport aircraft, two C-118s and a C-9 were inbound. The C-9 jet transport would be arriving first in one hour followed by the slower C-118s. I coordinated the buses for passenger pickup with the aircrafts' ETA.

Controllers within the tower moving metal noticed the continuing buildup of thunderheads to the west. Inclement weather could hamper the smooth operational flow hoped for during the reservists' arrival. Three buses show up for the C-9's pending arrival. Moisant Approach Control passed along the C-9 was forty miles west inbound. Radar indicated a huge cell of imbedded storms beyond the C-9. How would this impending weather affect the two remaining inbound transports?

Four Louisiana Air National Guard F-15s call for departure. AC2 Campbell advises them to hold short, while requesting an IFR release from departure control. Now twenty miles out, the C-9 will be making a radar-controlled approach to runway 04 as per approach control. Departure control released the flight of F-15s. Campbell advised the flight, "Jazz 66 flight, wind 050 at 8, maintain one zero thousand, contact departure, cleared for takeoff."

"Roger, switching."

Growing winds, from the storm to the southwest, mandated this C-9's approach would be the last before a runway change to accommodate the wind shift. The flight of F-15s began their staggered departure. Reaching a half mile beyond the departure end, each tipped their nose straight up, shooting toward ten thousand feet. Other than a spectacle to observe, no prior coordination had occurred, contrary to an existing letter of agreement for the immediate climb. The departure had caused chaos below on the surface also. One of Belle Chasse's food markets so happens to occupy property below their vertical ascent. Shockwaves busted out plate glass windows—community relations at its worst. I begin fielding calls from this fiasco while the first of the reservist air shuttles taxis toward the buses for off-loading. Obviously, noise abatement procedures aren't in sync with existing procedures.

Runway change completed with storms in the vicinity; approach control advised two C-118s will be arriving prior to the inclement weather's leading edge reaching the approach corridor. Bad vibe! Yes, ground-controlled radar approaches are available; heavy rain and wind downdrafts don't care—thunderstorms along the Gulf Coast, whether Corpus Christi or here at the mouth of the Mississippi River, any approach is dangerous. C-118s are notoriously slow, no way will they beat that approaching weather. Approach controller's prediction against my radar presentation didn't hold water. Old memories of "lost shipmates" locks in with a periodic flash warning, one I've learned not to ignore. Each C-118 is loaded with people, naturally concerned about the rough, wind-tossed approach they are experiencing. Any view out their porthole window surely wouldn't soothe their growing nervousness.

Five buses are lined up on the ramp's edge, barely visible from the control tower. Reduced visibility now hampers each pilot as they continue their precision radar approach looking for runway lights through the downdrafts of rain. Arriving in sheets, this type of hard rain associated with thunderstorms off the Gulf of Mexico generate wind shear—a disaster waiting to happen. On a two-mile final, the first C-118 experienced a loss of altitude from a strong downdraft which the pilot attempted to recover from.

"Golf Whiskey 544, Navy New Orleans GCA. Two miles from touchdown, below glidepath, slightly left of course turn right heading 224 degrees. Going farther below glidepath, well below glidepath. Pull up, your well below glidepath," the radar final controller firmly advised.

"GCA, Golf Whiskey 544. Roger, runway's not in sight, wind on final has downdrafts, we're pulling up and breaking off the approach. Wind shear at two miles."

Monitoring this approach, I knew the size of this rainstorm would cause the two transports to divert and land elsewhere, probably Moisant Airport on the other side of New Orleans. I quickly asked approach to confirm their intentions. All buses had to be rerouted toward New Orleans' civilian airport that would take, with the rain, an hour to arrive. Both C-118s diverted, choosing to arrive alive. The reservists would make it to the base for their weekend drills, just a few hours later than planned.

During his off-duty hours, Chief Leblanc hears of the delay and injects his nose into a situation already handled. I quickly tell him the situation, how it was controlled, and how low the first C-118 got before pulling up on final. Leblanc was making irrational statements. "Harper, you should have gone down to make the GCA approach." As if the qualified controller wasn't capable. "Standby after your shift in the morning for an AAR (after action review)." What a major-league douche-nozzle!

Next morning, I'm waiting for this ridiculous review Leblanc had mentioned. No one else knows anything concerning a review. Leblanc is missing. We find out he was arrested by base security that morning for inappropriate behavior with a neighbor's small daughter. The family living across the street from me had reported the situation last evening. Such a horrible ordeal upon one so young. I have a small daughter, and I live right next door. I drove home and had a discussion with my daughter. Thankfully nothing inappropriate had occurred toward her. The military moved quickly when proof was ascertained. We had new neighbors within two weeks.

AC3 Powell, a female controller demonstrating knowledge gleaned from manuals had now put some of that to use with a two-hour session involving medium to heavy intensity air traffic. She unplugged her headset as I put the finishing comments on an evaluation form and told her I was expecting a qualification recommendation from her section leader next week.

"Navy Tower, Moisant Approach. Inbound emergency, sixty miles south over the gulf is an SR-71 descending out of sixty thousand feet, call sign Blackbird One, lost an engine. Enroute your house in four minutes. WW."

"Moisant Approach, Navy Tower. Roger."

I tell the flight data operator to ring the emergency as I call the office below. Due to the top-secret classification of the SR-71, only certain eyes are even supposed to see the thing. Hopefully the fire chief at crash fire knows where to seclude this valuable equipment once it lands. News gets out, every coon-ass from Thibodeaux to De La Croix will want to see it and take a picture with it, top secret be damned. Procedures to follow here at NOLA with this type of emergency would surely be quite dusty; he had five minutes.

"Navy New Orleans Tower, Blackbird One is ten miles south for landing, single engine approach."

"Blackbird One, Navy Tower. Runway 04, length 8,000 feet, wind 020 at 8, check wheels down, cleared to land."

Thankfully, the crash captain had a follow-me truck along with other emergency vehicles escort the highly valued equipment to a closed-door hangar where it would be worked on in seclusion.

On the home front, dreams unwound. "Throwing It All Away," Phil Collins (1986). Divorce ensued. Colors faded to black and white. Was it too late to take those ship's orders out of Corpus Christi from a year and a half ago? You betcha. Warnings the USN had slapped my face way back in the PI, haunted sleepless nights. Maybe a bit too independent? Never. "We always did feel the same, we just saw it from a different point of view," Bob Dylan, "Tangled Up In Blue" (1975). Kids were worth it all, though. My relationship with the four children remained devoted and solid—greatest satisfaction came as I listened to my oldest daughter deliver her Belle Chasse High School Valedictorian speech. It was a validation of an intuitive hope, begun far away, across many bridges, under which a lot of water had flowed.

New Orleans' gumbo of blended cultures, different architecture styles, and variations of cuisine made it unique. My last day began with sadness from the impending emptiness without the kids in Oakdale; a sinking loneliness as placing flowers on a grave. Eating a last meal at the chow hall improved my outlook, realizing home cooking would be next. Mississippi River Bridge northbound; this river's muddy water flows through Louisiana with many twists and turns. Similarly, entering the navy twenty years before, I'd expected the same such path and life delivered. I'd joined the military in my own way, going off to fight Nixon's war. Along the way, I'd found my calling. "Oh, what a lucky man, he was," Emerson, Lake, & Palmer, "Lucky Man" (1970). Still, at thirty-nine, this USN retiree knew there were many rivers yet to cross. Time to leave my uniform behind and let my hair grow. Fair winds and following seas: January 29, 1993.

Fort Polk Army Airfield, Louisiana—February 1993

My second job required a sworn oath of allegiance as the first had, now as an army civilian working at Fort Polk Army Airfield for the next ten years. A major training facility both, for World War II and the Vietnam conflict—untold thousands of American men and women received vital information while training for warfare.

At work in the airport's operations office, I had just completed the necessary paperwork on a UFO sighting from an anxious observer who'd taken forty-five minutes on a phone call describing the account. I had first encountered such phone calls back in Lemoore Base Operations located in the San Juaquin Valley. Each call required soliciting information to determine if the call was a hoax or sounded legitimate. This information had been nationally compiled after research during the 1960s when investigations were conducted under a program called "Project Bluebook." Categories of UFO sightings were grouped as follows:

1.) Observed the UFO within 500 feet.
2.) Physical evidence was left such as skin burn, broken tree limbs, or radar sighting.
3.) Observed an alien form.
4.) Actual abduction.
5.) Communicated or interacted (verbally or telepathically) with this entity.

Whether these forms were ever authenticated by an investigation or thrown into the circular file, I can't answer.

Over the years, as nuclear power plants became common, more UFO reports began arriving at the closest military or civilian airports to where they occurred. These were valid concerns that people had a right to know. Other than a few phone calls made, any legitimate effort to investigate such cases would involve use of allocated funding earmarked for other projects. Most events of this nature were brushed aside, still ignorant of what could really be happening. Speaking up could be detrimental in more ways than one; AC3 Hinson perishing in a plane crash under the waters of the St. John's River in Jacksonville kept prickling my memory like a needle looking for a plump vein to penetrate.

Calls began arriving from a HALO drop zone miles away in a secluded area of Kisatchie National Forest. The calls involved an emergency which happened as the army rangers had a nighttime drop into a prepared landing zone cut out of the pine trees. The whole purpose being to drop a squad of parachutists from a more undetectable high altitude. This involves extended free-fall time prior to opening the chute just before landing in the drop zone. This extremely dangerous maneuver requires exact timing on pulling the rip cord. C-130 aircraft had picked up the rangers on the ramp here at the base prior to the jump commencing.

Post drop, Lieutenant Peart organized his squad just inside the drop zone. At 23:30 local time, Peart accounted for all members of the crew through night vision goggles, attached to his helmet, except Corporal Kelly. These goggles were a game changer for night-time combat situations. Though working as advertised, Peart still couldn't locate Kelly.

"Kennedy, Kelly preceded you out the aircraft…notice anything unusual?" Peart asked.

"No, sir."

"Line up every ten feet from drop zone's edge, let's make a revolving circle checking for Corporal Kelly."

SCUTTLEBUTT

Halfway through the search, Private Gibson stepped over a downed tree trunk, tripped, and fell on his back. Prior to sitting up, Gibson looked through the treetops as the waning moon temporarily whited out his vision through the goggles. Blinded for a couple seconds, a warm liquid dropped onto his lips. Before he could bring his hand up to wipe it away, his tongue darted out for a taste—warm and salty, like blood. Gibson jumped up, began spitting and wiping his lips on his sleeve. Shielding any glare with his hand, he looked up again into the huge canopy of a typical forest pine tree. The dawning realization knocked at the door to Gibson's frontal lobe as the previous thought left out the back. Trees bleed sap not salty blood. "Lieutenant Peart!" Gibson screamed, perhaps the loudest of his life.

Sixty-seven feet above the forest floor, the lifeless body of Corporal Kelly hung upright, impaled through his abdomen area with a tree's upper limb, long dead from a lightning strike. A tragedy not unheard of but rather spoken of only if necessary—the grisly nature, of course.

The major quake shuddering the American fabric on September 11, 2001, completely shut down all airspace in the US military components throughout the country awaited orders to respond, but to who? I processed flight orders for this contingency affecting Gulf Coast Air Defense Commands. Unlike any traditional threat, these heinous acts of terrorism seemed to have originated internally. Had any threats been picked up through intelligence channels? *Yes.* Had these threats been followed thoroughly and reacted upon? *No.*

Middle Eastern factions, once again influenced by religious zealots, acted out vengeful tactics against the large footprint the US had imprinted into the sands of that region. Both CIA and FBI centered their attention on Al Qaeda, a group of terrorists temporarily harbored in Afghanistan and protected by the Taliban. W unleashed the CIA. Amazingly successful in routing the Taliban, the small number of agents paid off warlords for assistance. Successfully using massive military bombardment, their only regret was allowing the top Al Qaeda terrorist leaders to somehow escape with Pakistani sympathizers.

This marginal victory was a positive step until the US pivoted into a disastrous sideshow of imperialism. Led around by the nose, W allowed another zealot on a mission—VP D. Cheney—to spearpoint a fabric of lies and deception upon the American people. "Let's create a rouse in the sand dunes, finishing the job your dad didn't—take out Saddam Hussein. We'll say he has mobile nuclear capability and was in cahoots with Al Qaeda. It'll be easy. They were pushovers in '91." Cheney had an axe to grind, needing only to hoodwink his boss and the rest of the country to do it. He succeeded. W was gullible enough to eat some of Cheney's convoluted word salad; most others grabbed a fork.

Within the crosshairs of Cheney and friends, Iraq became another blunder our government decided to make after refusing to learn the lesson of Vietnam. Young warriors, led down the primrose path, needed any help they could receive. I applied as a civilian air traffic controller at an army airfield on the Iraq-Kuwaiti border. Going in, I treaded choppy waters from within, working for a company sanctioned and utilized by the US government but under investigation for a whole slew of malfeasance. The guy responsible for us being in this predicament, the vice president had recently been the company's chief operating officer. The origin of a reoccurring sour taste I couldn't escape. Using abilities the government had trained me for, controlling aircraft, now for good salary, all the while paying Uncle Sam some more dues. I felt I couldn't help if I wasn't in the fight. They were the ones hiring—I bit.

Udairi Military Airfield Base, Iraq-Kuwait Border—August 2003

Turned fifty years old in 2003, ankle deep in the desert sands of a war zone rich in scorpions and wicked camel spiders. The army's aviation squadrons of attack and utility helicopters conducted missions against the Muslim factions of hate trying to keep the US out of their business. The desert on the Iraqi border with Kuwait is a harsh environment where mostly Bedouin nomads gather nightly under their tents. Just outside the protective berm surrounding the airfield, they grazed herds of camels, while weapons of war flew overhead to and from the battle. Fires from sabotaged oil fields kept night skies blazing while daytime, black smoke could be observed in the distance, creating massive environmental difficulties.

Civilian contractors working for KBR as myself, ran the logistics portion of the base. Some ran the chow hall, others base security, fueling depot, and airport control tower operations in my case. We had languished in Houston for over a month while KBR verified our applications, applied for our passports, and checked medical background. I'd had memorable conversations with men and women hoping to make "good money" driving truck convoys north. They were now learning how deadly the improvised explosive devices and roadside ambushes were, destroying those dreams. Never far from combat, convoys rolled north through Shiite controlled tracts of desert, crosshairs on each vehicle. Defensive escort helicopters were occasionally required, which the tower would launch on a moment's notice. Responsibility for the needed supplies therein were not taken lightly.

A steady moving line of grunts in fatigues and civilian contractors filed into the KBR managed chow hall centrally located in the base along the desert border. From the tap on my shoulder, I turned to see a familiar face behind. "Harper, I thought that hairy-looking dude up ahead was you. Company chow treating you right?" D. D. asked, placing his arm over my shoulder.

"Dizzi Diattawitz." I turn giving him a bear hug. "What is it, eight months? I've been hoping to lay eyes on you again."

Selecting the chicken cordon bleu, I waited for Dizzi as we headed into the noisy seating area. "It's a relief to see you, Diz. I really worry about you guys. Any word from Janice lately?" Janice was another contractor driving for KBR we'd met waiting for paperwork stateside. Dizzi set his tray on the table, looked me in the eyes, and said nothing. The implication stunned me. "Is she…?"

"Yes. Two months ago. Ambushed at a crossroads outside Nasiriyah."

"Dizzi, I talked to Janice a couple months ago in this chow hall before her convoy left."

"Lucky you got to see her before…it happened."

I pushed my tray of food away untouched. "She'd said her young daughter was staying with Janice's mother while she was earning them a way to the future."

Leaving the hall, I embraced Dizzi. "When's your departure time?"

"Half hour."

"Call your wife, talk to your kids…let 'em know you're here for them. Look me up right here next time."

"You got it, Harp."

Never saw or heard from Dizzi after that.

Previous US administrations had stumbled repeatedly for decades, when using force in the middle east. Religious sects actively opposing one another don't bode well for those establishing a governing body in a newly acquired country attained through war. Hundreds of thousands of beaten Iraqi soldiers were just simply released into the population—out of sight, out of mind kind of thinking or lack of thinking. US government created its own problems. If the consensus of people living in a captured country are religiously biased against their captors, any recipe will fail to win their support. Urban warfare, deadly for both sides, obliterated the civilian populace, their homes, and livelihood. We learned that badge on our chest, claiming to be the world's watchdog against civil wars or religious disputes, was a job the US was not good at nor could succeed in.

    I took some R & R exchanging desert sands for those on a beach. Flying over India and China, the beaches of Thailand, as the Philippines, were worth the effort getting there. Pristine oceanfront view with spectacular sunrises and sunsets nestled in palms and tropical settings. On a cue from a friend back in the desert, I arrived in Bangkok, eventually making it south through lush, green, tropic landscapes. I parasailed, zip-lined from hotel rooftops, snorkeled in pristine waters of Phuket, Thailand, the first week in December 2004, enjoying the beautiful island paradise which in three weeks would be swept away by a tsunami, killing hundreds of thousands throughout the region. Afterward, of course, mourning for the tremendous loss of life dominated human consciences worldwide. I couldn't help but remember the people living and working where I'd just returned from—were they victims? Extremely lucky and fortunate that I had one of the last adventures the area offered before nature reclaimed its old territory.

    Two years working with pilots, aircrews, and young soldiers departing the airfield, never to return alive; the sorrow became overwhelming. Once more, the defense of our homeland hadn't been on the table, yet massive blood loss resulted. Moral is, be careful who you vote for.

Troutdale Control Tower, Portland, Oregon—September 2005

Returning stateside after Katrina, amidst the toll the category 3 hurricane had heaped over New Orleans, I helped my family relocate toward a new home in California. Contract signed, I headed to a civilian airport in Portland, Oregon, of all places. I was elated; similar, I'd presume, to pioneers 150 years prior. Nestled between the Pacific coastline and the Cascade Mountain range on the south bank of the Columbia River, the area was a magnet for liberal-minded people concerned about their future and willing to discuss it responsibly. I was at peace. The joy of reading a local newspaper with editorials I agreed with; attending an environmental conference where climate change was recognized without blithering idiots challenging such notion; or simply taking the beauty of the Columbia River Gorge instilled tranquility.

Working in a civil aviation environment was different, but the same rules applied. The Portland business community kept the general aviation here busy. As pimples on a teenager's face, cone-shaped mountains populate the landscape's horizons, some active volcanos ready to pop. Mount Adams, Mount Hood, Mount Rainer just to name a few. Relying on visual reporting points, both pilots and air traffic controllers readily use mountains as checkpoints. Flowing through the valleys created by these mountains, the majestic Columbia River makes it way westward, cutting its path for millions of years into what is today referred to as the gorge, also the state boundary between Oregon and Washington. Just upriver from the airport on the Washington side is the Hanford Nuclear Power Plant. In addition to the ongoing environmental disaster on sight, people in the area continued making calls to authorities about sightings of unusual airborne phenomena.

Throughout years spent in the navy, occasionally, cases concerning UFOs rose to the surface only to be hushed up and mysteriously swept under some rug of "human complacency." Both the military and the FAA had supposedly more important things to be concerned with. How could that be? How could anything be more important than determining if an alien is flying doughnuts around you, probably laughing at our incompetence? Just doesn't make sense for our government to be that complacent; must be a cover-up. Any reasonable person would believe the most reliable source to receive a UFO report from would be the trained eye of a pilot, military or civilian. Becoming more evident year after year was the larger number of sightings around mountainous volcanoes or nuclear power plants. Hanford, Washington, was a case in point.

One hour into a two-hour stint on the local control position, I am busy with multiple aircraft in VFR touch-and-go pattern as well as a couple helos practicing landings to an unused taxiway. I received a call from a pilot upriver from the airport obviously in distress. "Troutdale Tower, Aztec 711 west of Hanford at five thousand inbound Portland. I'm encountering some type of object that's made two…" His transmission stopped.

"Aztec 711, Troutdale Tower. Last part of your transmission cut out, say again." No response. Within seconds, an emergency locator transmitter began its alarm over the tower's receiver. This indicates a plane is in serious trouble. I consulted with Portland Approach Control, telling them of the partial transmission received. A coast guard search and rescue helicopter begins a meticulous search of the last known position report the aircraft made.

Strewn down the side of a mountain leading into the gorge were the remains of the Aztec. The coast guard helo had no access to land. It had to lower its crewman with a hoist. The effort was for nought; only bits and pieces remained.

The National Traffic and Safety Board flew into the area to investigate. The hillside, though tough as hell to get to, did reveal the aircraft had fallen after a mid-air collision. Small pieces of one aircraft and one pilot littered the mountainside. If there was a mid-air, where's the other aircraft? Multiple parts of the littered remains of the aircraft had a mysterious red smudge, indicating whatever it hit was that color.

Investigation revealed in fact the aircraft had suffered a mid-air collision, but further evidence was inconclusive.

From the tower, the Columbia River, with Mount Hood dominating the backdrop, met the eye. To the north just across that river, sits Washington state, where less than fifty miles away, Mount St. Helens spews smoke plumes skyward on a weekly basis, reminding anyone who cares, "1980."

Smoke rising from atop Mount Hood was from a growing forest fire on the western slope. Firefighting helicopters had flown into the airport three days prior as a staging base to combat the growing flames. These copters were equipped with a deployable vacuum hose utilized to ingest then deploy water as needed.

"Blaze 03 and flight, Troutdale Tower, traffic Jetstream six mile straight in, depart southeast remaining east of the approach corridor, wind calm cleared for takeoff, report Crown Port outbound." Marsha unkeyed the foot pedal transmitter on the tower floor.

"Roger."

On ground control, I passed over the Jetstream's flight strip to Marsha. On watch since 7:00 a.m., we had rotated control positions every two hours. Typical in and outbound flights, with others wanting practice landings and departures here at the field, kept the pace flowing. From the get-go, crews manning the fire choppers continued departing and arriving at two-hour intervals; little rest for the weary.

Midmorning, I'm now working the local traffic pattern which overflies the Columbia River flowing westbound, still ten miles to Portland. Weather is CAVU, Clear and Visibility Unlimited, except one corridor where Mount Hood sits with its smoke restriction. N38464, a Cessna 210 on a cross-country flight plan from Spokane, checked in over Kelso, Washington, with a report of an ELT (Emergency Locator Transmitter). Tower radios receive these broadcasts from downed aircraft, but terrain surrounding the origin of the broadcast can inhibit reception. I passed along this info to other control agencies to scan for its source. All aircraft, currently on my radio frequency, was accounted for. Fire choppers switch from the tower frequency when they leave the five-mile airport area, then prior to reentry.

Climbing out of 200 feet, after refilling the helo's reservoir bladder with water from the Columbia River, Blaze 03 switched his radio frequency from his operating base back to Troutdale. "Troutdale Tower, Blaze 03."

"Blaze 03, Troutdale Tower, your transmission is broken and barely readable, go ahead."

"Tower, has Blaze 03B returned to base? I can't raise him on company."

"Negative, I do have a report of an ELT request you surveil your area."

"Rog."

Within twenty minutes, Blaze 03 reported the crash site of his flight member with GPS coordinates, requesting search and rescue. The tower helped facilitate rescue efforts to the sight. NTSB determined that after Blaze 03B had hovered over the Columbia River, its deployed hose sucking up the maximum its bladder could possibly take, the accident ensued. During the Sikorsky's lift, up and over the tall trees beyond the river's bank, compensation for the heavier load; more this pass than last, had been neglected somehow. Concern, alarm, terror, disaster, imminent death—all, surely, last thoughts of two brave firefighting air crewmen observing their last coherent view. Giant conifers were approaching through the canopy. Proving, in their own way, whether its military, police, firefighting, or search and rescue, that duty can involve loss of life. Be ready.

Crossing the Cascades as "pioneers" long before, a continuous flow of people created a demand on the housing market during '05 to '07. It had been my hope to finally settle in this area. Hope in one hand and face reality in the other. I was blindsided with a medical issue the unforgiving FAA medical board could not accept. Retirement reared its ugly head. Visiting a good chunk of this earth throughout twenty years in the USN took second chair to the satisfaction that working air traffic control brought.

Those two young boys I'd chased off the rooftops in Corpus Christi have travelled the Pacific and European theaters touring with their own band. Adam's Attic played their own music for US military components both at sea and isolated bases; what goes around, comes around.

"This was my life, it was my time, it was my world" (Ronnie James Dio), USN Chief Air Traffic Controller (Ret.) Jess Harper.

Works Cited

Adam's Attic. 2008.
Aerosmith. 1973. "Dream On." *Aerosmith*. Columbia.
Aerosmith. 1993. "Livin' On the Edge." *Get a Grip*. Geffen.
Allman Brothers Band. 1972. "One Way Out." *Eat a Peach*. Capricorn.
Allman Brothers Band. 1973. "Ramblin' Man." *Brothers & Sisters*. Capricorn.
Apocalypse Now. 1979. United Artists.
Bad Company. 1974. "Seagull." *Bad Company*. Swan Song.
Beach Boys. 1966. "Good Vibrations." *Beach Boys Good Vibrations*. Capitol.
Beatles. 1970. "Let It Be." Apple Records.
Bowie, David. 1973. "The Rise and Fall of Ziggy Stardust and the Spiders from Mars." RCA.
Collins, Phil. 1986. "Throwing It All Away." Atlantic.
Creature from the Black Lagoon. 1954. Universal International.
Deep Purple. 1972. "Smoke on the Water." *Machine Head*. Warner Brothers.
Demolition Derby. Mid-'60s. ABC Wide World of Sports. ABC.
Dio, Ronnie James. Biography. 2010.
Dirty Harry. 1971. Malpaso Company.
Doors. 1967. "Light My Fire." *The Doors*. Elektra.
Dylan, Bob. 1963. "Masters of War." *The Freewillin' Bob Dylan*. Columbia.
Dylan, Bob. 1975. "56th and Wabasha." *Blood on the Tracks*. Columbia.
Dylan, Bob. 1975. "Tangled Up in Blue." *Blood on the Tracks*. Columbia.

Emerson, Lake, & Palmer. 1970. "Lucky Man." *Emerson, Lake, & Palmer*. Cotillion.
Emerson, Lake, & Palmer. 1972. "From the Beginning." *Trilogy*. Island Records.
Harrison, George. 1970. "All Things Must Pass." *All Things Must Pass*. Apple.
Hendrix, Jimi. 1968. "All Along the Watchtower." *Electric Ladyland*. Reprise.
Hornsby, Bruce. 1986. "The Way It Is." *Bruce Hornsby and the Range*. RCA.
Jaws. 1975. Universal Pictures.
Jethro Tull. 1970. *Benefit*. Reprise.
Led Zeppelin. 1971. "Going to California" and "When the Levee Breaks." *Led Zeppelin IV*. Atlantic Records.
Led Zeppelin. 1973. "Houses of the Holy." Atlantic Records.
Lynyrd Skynyrd. 1974. "Freebird." *Lynyrd Skynyrd*. MCA.
Midnight Express. 1978. Casablanca Filmworks.
Night of the Living Dead. 1968. Image Ten.
Oldfield, Mike. 1973. "Tubular Bells." *Tubular Bells*. Virgin.
One Flew Over the Cuckoo's Nest. 1975. United Artists.
Osbourne, Ozzy. 1981. "Crazy Train." *Blizzard of Oz*. Jet, Epic.
Rolling Stones. 1968. "Sympathy for the Devil." *Beggars Banquet*. Decca.
Stewart, Rod. 1971. "Every Picture Tells a Story." *Every Picture Tells a Story*. Mercury.
Streets of San Francisco. 1972. Warner Brothers.
The Poseidon Adventure. 1972. 20th Century Fox.
Them. 1954. Warner Brothers.
Three Dog Night. 1967. "Mama Told Me Not to Come." *Eric Is Here*. MGM.
Toto. 1978. "Hold the Line."
Trower, Robin. 1974. "Bridge of Sighs." *Bridge of Sighs*. Chrysalis, Capitol.
Van Halen. 1982. "Runnin' with the Devil." *Van Halen*. Warner Brothers.
Victory at Sea. 1952. NBC.

About the Author

Raised in Louisiana, Bill Henry has spent thirty-four years in air traffic control around the globe. Now retired, his time is focused mainly between Tennessee and California.